Love Yoked Evenly For Ed

Author

Chelsea Songbird

Love Yoked Evenly For Ed
ADULT CONTENT

The characters and the story in this book are fiction.

www.chelseasongbird.com

Printed in the United States of America

All Rights Reserved

No part of this publication may be reproduced, stored in a retrieval system, or transmitted in any form, or by any means – electronic, photocopying, mechanical, recording, or otherwise without written permission from the author.

Copyright© 2019 by **CHELSEASONGBIRD PUBLISHING CO.**

Library of Congress Control Number: 2019933822

ISBN 978-0-9846217-3-6

ADULT CONTENT

Acknowledgments

This book is meant to open the eyes of all who are driven by only what they see. Life is deeper than what is on the outside of a person. You can fall in love with a monster if you only date eye candy. There is such a thing as hell on earth.

Forward

The United States of America was founded on the principles of freedom of religion. I was brought up to believe I had a choice, to believe whatever I wanted to believe, but I was influenced by my atheist parents. They always made fun of religion and people who believed.

The system created for the United States of America has lasted over two-hundred years. No other system in the world can compare to the freedom we have.

Ed, you opened my eyes to God and I thank you for doing that. I look at God and country in a completely different light now. My eyes are open to the importance of what America was founded on because now I know God, the Bible opened my heart.

'In God we trust' is printed on our paper money. I have a new appreciation for those words, spoken and printed by our forefathers. The song, 'God Bless America' is in my heart, sometimes when I hear it sung the feeling is so strong I well-up with tears.

I do not blame my parents for influencing me. My grandparents were also atheist and taught my parents their beliefs; I plan to break the generational curse and raise my children in the church.

Ed

Alice

www.chelseasongbird.com

Table of Contents

Chapter 1
Searching for Ugly

In the dictionary, the definition of ugly is 'displeasing to the eye; very unattractive.' This will be my answer for happiness in a relationship with my future wife. You see I am 27 years old and very lonely. Don't get me wrong, I have many friends, what I'm lonely for is a wife and family. I have out grown being with my buddies, running around doing whatever I want when I want. It is just boring, uninteresting to me now. That kind of life repulses me.

The reason I want an ugly woman for my wife is that I go crazy with beautiful women. First, I become insanely jealous of anyone who talks to them, then the fearful feeling that they will leave sets in because they become unhappy.

The last beautiful woman I had a relationship with I became envious of any man who even said hello to her. I would go into a rage and accuse her of wanting to be with them instead of being happy in our relationship. Nothing she could say would slow down my jealous heart, and my rage made the air heavy and thick with depression from my emotional state of mind. This was too much for her to deal with. She told me she loved me more than she loved anyone in the whole world, but I made her unhappy and she just could not live with my jealous heart. She left and I never heard from her again. I lost the love of my life and replaced her with drugs and alcoholic beverages. I felt this was the only way to deal with my loss. I just could not get her off my mind, and the fact that my behavior chased her away made it even worse.

Being drugged up all the time is not the answer to any problem. Drugs just make things worse. Your family and friends are the ones to suffer the loss of their loved one. A drugged up person just becomes a Zombie, wallowing in self-pity. Because of this selfish behavior, I lost several good years of my youth. I have been clean for five years now, but I will never get the years back that were wasted in a drug stupor.

I've dated many beautiful women and all have left me because I want to lock them in a room so other men cannot share their beauty. I can't even stand for other men to look at them. You see, beautiful women enjoy being looked at. That makes me a thief, because I steal their joy. I even become violent behind my controlling heart. The last beautiful woman I was with, brought out my violent side that I had no control over. Instead of making love to her, I was making hate to her by slamming my body into her and biting her lips instead of kissing her lips. This made her want to run from me, as if I was some sort of lunatic, a basket case. I find it strange how one wrong move can change everything for a lifetime, with women.

If a person cannot change, then perhaps changing the circumstances will fix the person. This is what I must try to do in order to find happiness in this ever-changing mind of mine.

I began my search for ugly in restaurants. First, I go into the restaurant during the lunch rush and sit at a table. I wait for an ugly girl to come in and I get behind her in line. I strike up a conversation about the weather, or some news story that everyone is aware of in this day and time. Then I ask if she would mind if I joined her for lunch. I tell her how I hate eating alone, and that she would be doing me a great favor, and how we would be freeing up a table for some other poor soul who would have to sit in their car to eat because, there would be no room for them in the restaurant. That makes two favors she would be doing in just one day.

This strategy works 90% of the time. Some 'ugly women' are just too shy and lack the confidence to share a conversation with an extremely handsome man. In case I forgot to mention, I have a million dollar smile and a build like few men will ever possess, even those who live in a gym. God blessed me with good looks and this is why beautiful women throw themselves at me all the time. They soon find out that handsome is only skin deep when I lock them away from the world.

Today I see the perfect woman entering the restaurant and I immediately get behind her in line. She has long brown hair and is overweight by about 50 pounds. Her nose is too long for her face, but she has kind eyes. Her clothes are baggy to hide the bulges of fat that ripple underneath. She has a triple chin that makes it look like she has no neck. She is perfect. I give her 'the line' and she falls for it hook, line, and sinker.

We find a table near a window with just two chairs. As the light hits her eyes, I see them twinkling with excitement. It makes me feel good to bring this kind of joy into someone's life.

She stretches out her hand and says, "My name is Alice." As I reach across the table, I feel her vibe before I ever touch her hand. "My name is Ed, pleased to meet you," I said. When our hands touched, the feeling was stronger than any woman has ever transmitted with just a handshake. It was like fireworks. As she tried to draw her hand back, I gripped it so the feeling could last a little longer. While still holding her hand I asked if she was dating anyone and in the same breath let her know I noticed she was not wearing a wedding band.

"Actually I haven't dated in over a year. Somehow, the guys I meet are dead beats. They expect me to take care of them and all I want out of life is a 50-50 relationship. I'm 25 years old and I have never been in a healthy relationship. I'm not giving up or anything like that; I'm just not going to date anyone that wants me to take care of them. I'm going to know more about the person I date before I waste any more valuable time and possible heartache on them," Alice said.

She ended her little speech with a giggle and a sly look out of the corner of her eye. I think this is just the Ugly I've been looking for. She has a head on her shoulders, and men that would be competition for me would never give her a second look. She's perfect.

"If you're not busy tonight I would like the opportunity to take you to a movie. We seem to think a lot alike. I have a good job, so you won't need to take care of me, and I have my own place and car. I like your personality and would like to get to know you better," I said.

Alice just looked at me with her fork full of corn about to enter her mouth, and gently lowered it back on her plate. Alice began to blush and her eyes were avoiding contact with mine. I reached across the table to give comfort to an uneasy feeling I could see in her demeanor. As I reached across the table, the vibe once again filled my body, and by the time I touched her arm I was melting like a stick of butter. The touch was heavy with a light tingling metallic sound only the two of us could hear. It is one of those moments that will stay with you for a lifetime.

Alice slowly focused her eyes on mine and said, "Are you serious, you are such a handsome man and I'm, well just look at me, I'm not in your league. Won't you be embarrassed to be seen with me?"

"You underestimate yourself Alice, I guess you just dated one too many bums. Let me take you out and your confidence will resurface," I said.

4

Alice once again picked up her fork and with a nod to indicate a yes, began to eat. We both felt the chemistry between us and words were not necessary. We exchanged phone numbers and agreed on what movie we would go see. This could very well be the woman I will spend the rest of my life with. Right now ugly is beautiful. I haven't been this excited about a date since I was in High School. I feel like a kid again.

As I thumb through my clothes trying to figure out what to wear, a pink shirt catches my eye. I haven't worn this shirt but once; it was a gift from my mother. When I look at this shirt, I see the pink blush on Alice's cheek when I asked her out. That gives this shirt new meaning and now, right this minute, it is my favorite shirt. This should make my mom happy; she always asks why I don't wear it. This pink shirt will go good with my faded blue jeans with the brass button-up fly and a frail hemline. Now not only do I feel like a teenager, I look like one.

The movie theater is inside a mall and we agree to meet at 6:00 p.m. in front of the popcorn machine. Alice wanted it this way until we get to know each other better; it's called "Going Dutch". You each pay your own way.

As I approached the popcorn stand, I stopped and just watched Alice as she looked right and then left as if she wasn't sure I would make it to our "Dutch" date. I decided to call her cell phone just to hear what she sounded like on the phone and to calm her down.

"Hello, this is Alice," said Alice. "Hello, this is Ed and you look lovely tonight. Where are your glasses? I almost didn't recognize you. I love your pink outfit. We will look like twins tonight," I said.

"Where are you? I'm looking all around but I don't see you," Alice said.

"Look up and to your right. I'm on the second floor," I said.

"I see you. Pink becomes you; with all those muscles it gives you a soft touch. Are we going to talk all night on the phone, or are we going to the movie?" Alice said.

"I'm on my way, if you haven't picked a movie yet, there is a romance story I would like to see, that is if it is alright with you?" I said.

"Hang up the phone and get down here, we don't want to be late. I love romance stories," Alice said.

"You know pink is a soothing color. Some football programs paint the visitors' locker room pink to take the edge off their opponent. I wore it today to keep my cool and to match the blush on your cheeks when you were embarrassed at lunch. Pink so becomes you," I said.

"You're making me blush right now. You know Ed, the reason I asked to meet you here instead of letting you pick me up is that I thought you would not show up, and this way I could at least go to a movie to lick my wounds. You are so handsome and I'm so, well just look at me compared to you," Alice said.

"If there is one thing I have learned in this life, it is that beauty is only skin deep. Alice you are beautiful on the inside, and that, time can't wrinkle and steal from you. Your heart makes you beautiful to me, and your touch is more beautiful than anything I've experienced in my life. You have no idea what a gift you are." I said.

"Are you always this expressive with women you hardly know?" Alice said.

"I feel like I've known you all my life, it's for sure I've been looking for you all my life," I said.

As we walked hand in hand a striking woman with long blond hair, sky blue eyes, dressed to the hilt in platform high heels that matched her eyes, looked at me and smiled like she knew me. Without thinking, I nodded and smiled back at her.

Alice dropped my hand and coldness filled the air.

I immediately realized the effect this has made on her. I recognize myself in her. This is what happens to me when a man notices the woman that I am with. With Alice, I'm safe from this feeling, but Alice will feel jealous if she can't control my need to look at beautiful women. It's a man thing, noticing beautiful women. It's like women noticing a pretty flower or pretty dress. They just appreciate the beauty. It's the same thing.

Somehow, I must explain to Alice that men have this visual thing when it comes to women. It's natural, automatic when a beautiful woman is present to notice her. In my opinion, only around 10% of women fall into this category. In other words, it just does not happen that often. However, it did just happen, and on our first date. If Alice warms back up, I will address this the next time it happens.

I give it some time and make small talk about the posters for coming attractions. This goes on for some time. I check my watch and it's time for us to get in the theater for the movie is about to begin. I grab Alice's hand and head for the door.

"We better get moving, it's time for the previews to start," I said.

"You're right, time flies when you're having fun," Alice said.

I gave her hand a squeeze and the warm feelings were coming back slowly. I let Alice pick where she wanted to sit and we wound up at the top row, dead center, which is where I would have picked myself. We had no one around us; this gave us a certain amount of privacy. I feel really good about Alice.

The movie is full of drama and the characters have no control over their hormones. Strong attractions are being emitted from every character and it is as if they are in this bubble of intense feelings and the bubble is about to burst because it is unable to contain all the emotions being released by the actors.

The movie is about three couples who are all extremely good looking and all are somewhat attracted to one another. The attraction is not only physical but mental as well. They all have a great sense of humor complemented by a set of high moral standards. Their morals are what keep them from intruding on each other's partner. The whole movie plot is the restraint they practice that keeps them from entering into each other's relationships. They each discipline their action so not to cross the invisible line of strong emotion created by the rush of hormones. Youth has a way of stirring up these hormones. Humans must control the temptation of what is natural with the birds and the bees.

One of the couples controls their feelings with their obedience to God's law. They admit their attraction for their friends to each other and both refuse to let the snake bite them. They are both so aware that these feelings can occur throughout their entire life, and they refuse to become a victim of loss of control.

Another couple refuses to damage the relationship of their good friends with deception of their trust for one another when they are out of sight. In other words, they value their friendship over their hormones.

The last couple is struggling to find control over the visual effect that a bathing suit has on them. The eye candy is so powerful; they constantly put the friendships at risk. Their wondering eyes do not go unnoticed. These two put an edge on the movie. Everyone wonders when they will fail.

As the movie unfolded, the whole plot was to find a way for the couple that struggled to control the effects of their hormones, and find a solution to their problem. This was openly discussed on the boat right after everyone just took a dip in the water. It was a very vulnerable time for six people with perfect builds and beautiful faces.

The scene in the movie that I can most relate to is when one of the male stars said to another male star, "I can understand you looking at this beautiful woman on my arm, what I can't understand is the lingering look you are giving her. You are insulting me." I so understand that statement.

As the movie progressed, I felt like I was in a therapy session. The female star that was struggling with keeping her control, had a tendency to try to bend down in front of the men every chance she got, to show off her breasts in her swimsuit. She is very well endowed and the guys can't help but look. The other two women finally get through to her that she was very insulting to them and she quit flaunting herself. Her excuse was that her boyfriend was looking the other girls over and this is how she handled her jealousy with a "back at you" attitude. She now understands this is destructive behavior and it hurts the other girls more than it bothers her boyfriend. He rather liked watching the whole scenario.

About the time everything became normal, for the three couples and the rude behavior had stopped, a boat with two other couples pulled up beside them. These four people are also beautiful people and they are on a yacht. The yacht is five times larger than the boat and one of the guys invited the three couples to come aboard and have some refreshments.

They tied the boat to the yacht and boarded. Refreshments were served and a lot of small talk took place. The problem couple started their games again but only with the two couples on the yacht. Their friends were spared the rude behavior.

When everyone returned to the boat and the yacht sailed off on the clear blue water, the problem couple simply said, "We can't stop forever in just one day. Anyway you all are safe from our fun."

He calls it fun. Their reckless fun causes others a lot of pain. Someday their little game will backfire on them. You just can't romance everyone who is beautiful without falling for one of them eventually. That is when their pain will begin. They will lose each other.

As we exited the theater Alice said, "That's the way it is in Hollywood, California, hardly any of the beautiful people stay together for very long. Some say that beauty is a curse, because other beautiful people are always tempting them. I think I'm safe but I don't know about you."

I said, "Thank you Alice, I will take that as a compliment. I agree with you that it can be a curse, if you let it be."

The theater is emptying quickly and I grab Alice's hand and ask if she would like to get a cup of coffee and a piece of pie. The mall has a nice restaurant and since we drove separate cars this will work out for both of us. Alice agreed and I gave her hand a squeeze with excitement.

We both had a piece of cherry pie and black coffee. We made a lot of small talk about the movie before things began to get serious.

Alice asked, "What makes a handsome man like you ask an overweight homely girl with a big nose like mine, out for a date? Why aren't you with someone in your own league? I hate to be so blunt, but even in the movie we just saw, everyone was evenly matched. Aren't you embarrassed to be seen with me? I see how people look at us. It's like, what goes with those two? I don't mean to put you on the spot but I need to know what's going on."

I responded with, "First of all you underestimate yourself. You have a way about yourself that makes you beautiful. There is a lot to the statement that beauty is only skin-deep. I know many beautiful people who are ugly to the bone. It doesn't take long to find that out about the beautiful self-centered people roaming this earth. They seem to want to share their beauty with everyone. I'm looking to date someone who doesn't crave attention all the time from the outside world. I want to be their only world."

Alice said, "I definitely fit that mold. No one ever

looks at me as beautiful. You are safe there. My mother always told me that beauty is an attention getter in the beginning, but after a while, you don't even notice. She would compare beauty of a person to a beautiful work of art that you hang on your wall. You may go years without even noticing it, and someone comes along and makes a comment about how beautiful it is, and you say, 'yes it is.' In other words, beauty is nice, but it becomes just part of the wall, you never notice after awhile. She has a point you know."

I said, "She is spot on. I've never heard it put so clear. It makes perfect sense. Beautiful women have been my downfall all my life. I go crazy when other men look at them and I want to lock them up so I don't have to deal with my crazy mind. In fact, I did just that with the love of my life. She could not handle the isolation and left me because of it.

I created my own hell because of my jealous heart. I chased away the love of my life. Darkness surrounded my life, and I reached for drugs to bring back a spark of happiness. They are the biggest lie of all because after a while they take away every good thing you ever had and the darkness intensifies to the point that it is unbearable. I became a drug addict. I didn't care about my family, about vacations, about even taking a bath. It was hell on earth. Being an addict is like your drowning and you are trying to swim to the surface for air, your air is the drug. That's how powerful the need for the next fix is. You are empty inside and only the drug can fill you up. It's a vicious cycle.

I did not know if I could ever fix myself. My family stepped in or I would be six feet under today. That's how bad it was.

My little brother Jeff was playing football and he received a violent blow to his head, which caused a concussion. He was wearing my old football helmet to bring him luck. It was faulty and cracked right where his brain injury occurred. This is the first time I felt anything in two years. Watching my little brother lay in that bed, not knowing if he would ever open his eyes again got my attention.

He had a mad crush on this girl from Oklahoma named Chelsea Songbird. This little girl had seen my desperate need to talk to Jeff, and right there in the hospital asked the family to join hands around Jeff's bed, and make a pact to get me off drugs. It was an intervention, and thanks to Chelsea Songbird, I've been clean from drugs for five years, and never plan to do them again. The ironic thing about all this, is when Jeff came out of his coma, he did not have a clue about who Chelsea Songbird was. He felt odd when she was around. I've taken little brother under my wings and have taught him how to comb his hair and tie his shoes. He has come a long way now and is ready to claim his independence. I'm moving on with my life and you are the first date I've had in five years."

Alice said, "That's a lot of information about you. I'm just drinking it in. Forgive me if I seem distant, I need to digest all this and see if I'm strong enough to be a part of it all. I wouldn't want to be a reason for you to backslide into drugs again. After all you did blame it on a woman."

I said, "It's not the woman's fault that she is beautiful, it's my fault for not knowing how to handle the situation. I would not blame her, you, or any woman. I blame only myself. Don't worry; I will never do drugs again. Drugs will never steal my freedom again. I didn't like that feeling of when you are starving and desperate to feed yourself, and only drugs could fill you up. That's all behind me now. I would leave you before that would ever happen.

I'm just looking for someone to share my life with. It may not even be you. That's something that takes time. I just know that I like being with you, and would like to take you on a date, not just meet you for a movie. I want to get to know you better. I refuse to worry about what you think of me, that's why I'm sharing my history with you. Worry only makes me uncertain about the world and generates more problems. I'm your open book and you can read any chapter in this book.

For some reason I wanted to control others behavior, I just didn't get it's that I am only responsible for my behavior. Other people's behavior is just none of my business. I need to understand the meaning of unconditional love.

I now live one day at a time since I lost the love of my life five years ago. I need to learn to take care of myself and if a woman wants to stay with me, great, and if she wants to leave me for someone else, I must accept that and move on with my life.

I have a right to be angry if other men look at her longer than I think is acceptable, but I don't have a right to physically keep her away from everyone she cares about. My needs were so much more important to me than her needs were to her. Her freedom to be herself just didn't matter to me. I know how wrong I was, my eyes are open now.

God will give back what Satan has stolen, all I have to do is ask. God said he would put his law in my heart and mind, Hebrew 10 'I will be merciful, your sins I will remember no more.'

If God can forget I was a drug addict, then so can I. You can only become what God wants you to be by letting the Holy Spirit take over your mind. That's where I'm at right now. If I live my life to please God, I will find joy. We are all sinners; to be conscious of the Holy Spirit helps guard us from committing sins against ourselves."

Alice said, "I think you will be safe as far as other men looking at me, it seldom happens. This should help you with that problem. I never hold the past over anyone, I learned that from my mom, however if you go back to the world of drugs, I'm out of here. If it doesn't come from a doctor, I don't approve. Self-medicating is dangerous business and I want no part of it. I will just disappear out of your life, no need to tell you so you can try to stop me. Also, your addiction to beautiful women in my presence must stop. When you saw a beautiful woman while we were walking to the movie, and you made a gesture to let her know you noticed her, I felt insulted. When you are with me, you are with me only. What you do without me is your business.

Because I look the way I do, I'm hypersensitive to other people's gestures. If that lady would have acknowledged my existence, I might have felt different. It was as if she slapped me in the face. You are a very handsome man and women will always look at you with interest. What I'm asking is that you realize how it makes me feel."

I said, "I'm so sorry. You are right, it won't happen again. I get a little buzz when it happens and it has become a habit. I'll work on that.

I would not wish what happened to me on anyone. You see I'm hypersensitive to any man looking at the woman I'm with. When the woman I would be with responded to the man's gestures, there was a thick deep darkness that filled my body, its called depression, brought on by jealousy. Alice, I will never make you feel that way again. I understand.

What happened to me will never happen to you because of me. For me, I thought the drugs would chase away the darkness until I was strong enough to deal with my loss; instead, I just sank deeper and deeper into the darkness. Everything bothered me, even the breathing of a loved one was like fingernails on a chalkboard. It's like I punished my entire family with alienation. That's no way to treat the people who love you.

I've put a plan in place that will assure me the drugs will never take my life away from me again. The things that cause me mental anguish are being eliminated from my life. Beautiful women will be something I will admire from a distance. I will never put myself in harm's way due to my lust for beauty. I'm going to control my environment.

I understand your concern that I may return to the drug induced stupor I lived in for many years, but I assure you that is all in the past. I hated that lifestyle, but addiction would not let me out. I now know addiction, as I know the face of the devil. Darkness is evil.

Good looks can be a curse if you let them. People just want to be around beauty, the good and the bad. Sometimes beauty can make the good turn bad. I'm a good example of that. I lacked the ability to deal with my lust. I was young and powerful feelings were upon me. I now have the knowledge to deal with my emotions. Look but don't touch.

I read the Bible daily for the answers on how to live my life. The first words in the Bible are, 'Let there be light,' Genesis. Yet it was the fourth day before the sun was created. The Bible is talking about the light of God, a spiritual light. I've replaced the darkness of the devil with the light of God and this is why I know drugs will never be a part of my life again, you can be sure of this. Alice you will not dump me because of drugs, I can assure you of that."

Everything became quiet. I gave Alice an out by saying the word, 'dump'; it's a very powerful word that most everyone has experienced. I wanted to be sure that she knew she could get out of a relationship if she felt that we were not right for each other. Being dumped is very painful and for this reason, both parties should exercise caution.

An ugly girl can hurt you just as much as a beautiful woman, but they are less likely to because they are more grateful to be in your presence.

Alice said, "I appreciate your bluntness. I totally agree with the Bible being a good source to live your life by, light-heartedness is much more appealing than a dark cloud over ones head, that's what people say about the Bible. I haven't read it.

You need to know that I haven't dated a lot. You may have to show me the ropes, and I kind of wear my heart on my sleeve. That can be hard to deal with. I promise to work on it."

If that is all the problems this girl has, then I think we have a good chance of having a healthy relationship. I really like her personality and that is the most important thing for me, now that my eyes are open. I want to feed my mind not my eyes.

Alice is very upfront with her demands and I like that. There is no trying to figure out what she is thinking. She's in your face with her feelings. A miracle is a breach of the natural order and that may very well be what Alice is, a miracle meant for me only. I don't have to guess what she is thinking, like I do with beautiful women, and that makes me secure with Alice. It's a great feeling.

I realize the mistakes I've made will haunt me when I grow old and I don't want any more major mistakes in my life. In my world of drugs, I became calloused, cold, and no longer responded to love of any kind. In a drug stupor, I forgot how to give or even receive love and affection. I think Alice can get me back to living again. I'm willing to take a chance on her.

Alice said, "It's getting late Ed and I have to get up early in the morning. Would you mind walking me to my car?"

I said, "I wouldn't have it any other way."

As we walked to the car, a thought came into my mind about what my dad had told me when I was ten years old. He said, "Don't judge a book by looking at its cover." He had to explain when I asked him what book he was talking about. Anyway, until now I never put much stock into that wise statement. I looked at women for their beauty when I asked them out on dates. If they weren't drop dead gorgeous I did not even give them the time of day. That is just how my mind works. This is the first date I've ever had with an ugly woman and it is great. If I had listened to my dad, I could have saved all those lost years of self-pity in a drug induced stupor.

Chapter 2
The Next Day

Sunday morning came rushing through the window brighter than I've seen it since I was a kid. A thrill filled my body as I removed the sleep from my eyes. Was my date with Alice still lingering in my body, giving me energy and a brightness that is surging from head to toe?

Jeff knocked on my bedroom door and said, "Breakfast is ready, we don't want to be late for church."

I grabbed my robe, slipped into my slippers, and began singing at the top of my lungs. As I opened my bedroom door, Jeff looked me in the eye with a smile on his face.

Jeff said, "You must have found her last night. I can feel her in the air. She has definitely improved your disposition. Normally you come through that door all grumpy asking 'where's the coffee,' bumping into chairs, and when you finally sit down you put your face into your hands and start falling asleep at the table. If I must say so myself, this is a welcome change to your disposition."

I said, "Little brother, this is the one. We could set in this house all day and never say a word and I would be happy. You see little brother we can feel each other, and words are not necessary. That is what this girl can do for me."

Jeff said, "What is her name and when can I meet her?"

I said, "Soon. Her name is Alice and she is 25 years

old, never been married and hasn't dated anyone in a year. There are no past lovers, so I could in the very near future be her first love and hopefully her last love."

Jeff said, "Wait a minute, you just met this woman. To make her your lifelong love you need to be sure you know just who she is, and if she is the person she is portraying herself to be."

I said, "I know you've heard the old saying 'love at first sight,' well this is, 'love at first touch,' much stronger and longer lasting. In my life, no one has made me feel like I do at this very moment. Beauty is in the eye of the beholder, and I tell you Jeff, this is the most beautiful woman I've ever known."

Jeff said, "Ed, I would hate to see you slip back into that dark world that you lived in for so many years because of another beautiful woman."

I said, "Little brother, you know that will never happen to me again, I have God in my heart, and as of yesterday, I have Alice in my heart; a gift God gave me."

Jeff just shook his head, handed me the cup of coffee, and headed for the shower. I went to the back yard, grabbed a chair and began sipping my coffee. The mind is a wonderful thing when you hand it over to God. It can fill your body with so much pleasure and happiness that you can feel like you are busting at the seams. Two days ago I did not feel like this, now my mind has found love and my heart is making my body feel wonderful. Drugs can't touch what I'm feeling, and love is free. It just doesn't get any better than this.

Jeff said, "The shower is all yours, I'm going to get dressed now."

When we get in church, I'm going to thank God for bringing Alice into my life. He is all that is good, and so is my new life, thanks to Him. Heavenly light shines on my face now, not natural light, but God's light; there is a difference. There is something refreshing about you when you have God inside.

My little brother Jeff brought God back into my life. Before I set out on my journey to find a wife, Jeff asked if he could tell me what his views were on love. It went something like this, 'To me love is giving unselfishly of oneself, and giving that person the ultimate friendship. Love is saving sex for the very special person you plan to marry. It takes a powerful person to be abstinent. If you can do this you can keep yourself healthy, both physically and emotionally.' As I wash my hair, I wonder if Alice has ever been sexual with a man. Could I be her first? Love is not a word that falls easily from my lips, but I'm shouting in the shower, "I love Alice."

As we walked into the church, I greeted people with a realness I did not possess just the week before. The people could feel it and their responses were more intense. I could see it in their faces.

As the preacher gave his sermon, one of the verses he touched on really hit home. 'Real help comes from God,' Psalm 3:8. My heart melted when he said those words.

I begin to imagine myself and Alice standing at the front of the church and this very pastor asking if I will take Alice to be my lawfully wedded wife. I pull her white veil from her face and kiss her on the mouth and say, "I do."

Alice is God's gift to me, I know this, I can feel this. I will do everything in my power to keep her happy.

As the services ended and we walked out of the church, one of the parishioners said to me, "Ed, you have a little twinkle in your eye, where did you get it from?" I responded, "God gave it to me."

Everyone is heading to the parish hall where we will exchange stories, drink coffee and eat a donut or two. A couple named Joe and Mary sat at our table and introduced themselves. They know Jeff because he has attended this church all his life; I joined recently. They are a pleasant couple and the conversation started out light but moved into a deep dark conversation.

Mary left the table to talk to some female friends she had not seen in a while. Joe began to tell Jeff that he had heard rumors that Mary is seeing another man on the side. You see, Joe and Mary are engaged to get married in six months. He does not believe a word of it but does not know how to ask Mary about it or how to stop the vicious rumors.

Jeff said, "Sounds like the work of the Devil. One of his favorite sins is character assassination. I just can't see Mary doing anything like that. If she did it would probably be just a little slip, if she wanted him she would be with him, now wouldn't she? The person spreading all these rumors is either jealous of what you and Mary have, or they want to break you two up so they can move in and take one of you for their self. There are a couple of passages in the Bible that will help you with this situation. They go like this, 'A perverse man spreads strife, and a slanderer separates intimate friends,' Proverbs 16:28. Another passage goes like this, 'He who conceals hatred has lying lips, and he who spreads slander is a fool. Hatred stirs up strife, but love covers all,' Proverbs 10:18

Joe, if you believe God's promises, then you never need to worry about what life will bring your way. You are wasting precious time on earth. I suggest you forget about what the Devil is trying to do, and let God handle it. Don't hurt Mary with someone else's lies. Just forget you ever heard it."

I said, "If I may add to this conversation a word of wisdom, it would be, sowing discord among the brethren is the same as gossip. I've been studying the Bible and came across my now favorite verse. "Those six things the Lord hates, yes seven are an abomination to Him: A proud look, A lying tongue, hands that shed innocent blood, a heart that devises wicked plans, feet that are swift in running to evil, a false witness who speaks lies, and one who sows discord among brethren," Proverbs 6:16-19.

Satan led a third of the angelic creations into his rebellion against God. Satan and his demons want each and every one of us. Don't let him and his demons ruin your love for Mary. Pride is what caused Lucifer to fall from Grace and become Satan. We must seek the will of the Lord, not our will. I know you want to confront Mary with all this bad stuff, but remember, she will never forget that you believed the lies being told about her. She will feel creepy by what you say. Do you want this hanging over your marriage?"

Joe said, "You are right. I'm going to get down to the bottom of this and find out what demon is spreading these rumors and put an end to them. From now on I'm going to let faith be my sixth sense, as it says in Romans 14:23, 'Whatever is not from faith is sin,' and Hebrews 11:6 'And without faith it is impossible to please Him.' God gave me Mary and I put my faith in Him. My father always told me, 'You can either live in the spirit or live on your own. Jealousy is a bitter emotion that will eat you alive.' The reason I wanted to ask Mary about the rumor is because it put a jealous seed in my heart to think she would be with another man. I wanted to rid myself of that feeling at her expense. I'm so glad I talked to you two about this situation. Thank you for your advice."

Jeff said, "Let God fight your battles and you will always win. The Bible is a reliable source of knowledge in finding happiness, use it. You can't rely on the complexities of the mind, however, you can rely on the Bible. We have to go, will you tell Mary goodbye for us?"

What just happened was amazing. We just saved a precious relationship from being tainted with jealousy. The devil's evil nature lets him be known as the accuser, Prince of demons, the evil one, father of lies, and the deceiver, all which are negative. We just kicked the devil's butt and it feels great. The purpose of a demon is to destroy you with his wicked power; I'm so glad I can now see a demon for what he is.

I said, "You know Jeff, I learned firsthand that paranoia of your woman looking at another man brings pain and blinds what is real. It results in a tragedy of a lost relationship and unhappiness. It feels so good to save a relationship. The human mind is the most powerful gift God gave humankind. For me, jealousy is the most vehement flame filled with pain, and it burned my mind to ashes. Thanks to you and me, Joe won't have to go there."

Jeff said, "Makes you feel good to stop evil, doesn't it. We saved Mary's honorable reputation by guiding Joe in the right direction. We saved him a lot of money by keeping him from having to go to counseling to keep his and Mary's future marriage trouble free. If not for our words of wisdom, they would be going through intense psychological probing into their love relationships with a marriage counselor who would never mend the damage done by mistrust. If you don't let anyone steal your brain with their lies, you should have a healthy marriage. Always let your brain get its food from the Bible. It always has the right answers to any question. You can trust Jesus because he gave his life for you. If you let Jesus take control of your thoughts, He will replace bad thoughts with good thoughts."

I said, "Little brother you are spot on. I tried counseling when me and Lucy were having our problems and got nowhere. Pain and anger go hand in hand. I could see through Joe's head as if it was a glass fish bowl. I was Joe at one time. The emotional consequences can be devastating when depression and guilt set in from trying to control your woman. We saved Joe a lot of heartache today."

On the drive home from church just mentioning Lucy's name brought back memories of how insane I was because of her. I was mortified when any man just looked at her. Now that I'm cured of my jealous heart, I can see how miserable I made Lucy. I'm a thief who stole her happiness. Mental sickness caused from jealousy makes a monster rear its ugly head like a sickness that destroys the soul. I hope Satan did not plant a seed in Joe's brain that will destroy his love for Mary. I hope we reached him in time.

Lucy is in my past and I intend to keep her there. The love of my life is Alice and now that I'm home, I'm going to sit in the back yard and give her a call. Just dialing her number is making me all giddy. I'm like a high school boy with his first crush.

The phone rings five times and I'm about to hang up when Alice answers. "Hello Alice, how are you?" I said, "I'm beginning to think I'm telepathic, I was thinking how nice it would be to hear your voice right when you called."

I responded, "I go perfect with you, better than any other man on earth."

Alice said, "Slow down. You are shocking me in a good way; I just want to keep my head on straight until we get to know each other better."

I said, "I've kicked open a lot of doors in my time but I want this one to open on its own. I just want you to know how I feel. I don't want some other man to sweep you off your feet without you knowing how I feel about you. Your beauty has elevated my spirit and I can't hold it back. The touch of your hand creates such delight and I'm desperately trying to express my renewed enthusiasm for life all because of you. Before I met you, I was like a raindrop in the ocean, I felt unimportant. The moment I met you I began to matter again. When I woke up this morning I began singing songs and putting your name in each of them. After church today, I helped a young man put his jealous heart on a shelf, and show his soon to be bride his good side. My heart explodes with joy knowing this couple will be spared the pain jealous hearts create. When you center your life around yourself, you rob others of the joy you could be sharing, the pure enjoyment of one another's company. They possess beautiful youth with adorable passionate love that must not be spoiled with a jealous heart. If you've been there it's easy to explain and the young man got the picture.

I want you to know Alice; this is the best day of my life. I'm experiencing pulsating joy that is endless. I no longer can tell the imagined from the real, I'm so at peace with you in my life. When can I see you again?"

Alice said, "I'm bashful and without much confidence, but I do feel what you feel when you touch my hand and it is mighty powerful. Only time will tell if it is a lasting feeling and I need to take it slow. Your flirtatiously wooing with a hint of innocents has my head swimming. You are way out of my league and I could be in for the ultimate heartache."

I said, "Not a chance. I know myself very well and you are the girl of my dreams, I would never hurt you physically or emotionally. I need to see you as soon as possible. I'm bursting at the seams with the joy you give me."

Alice said, "Let's meet for dinner tomorrow night at 7:00 p.m. You know that French restaurant on Third and Bryant, they have really good food and their prices are reasonable, we can go Dutch."

I said, "Perfect, I will try to keep control of my emotions, but I make no promises. Good night till tomorrow."

I listen to her story with compassion in my heart, I could feel what she was feeling, I could hear with my heart. I sense a heavy burden that Alice thinks she may take a big fall into heartache land. I hope she takes the big fall, but I will never break her heart.

Chapter 3
Dinner

As I dress for my Dutch date with Alice, thoughts cross my mind about every girl I've ever dated, one thing they all had in common is their beauty. Lust drew me to them.

My feelings for Alice are so different. They have a light and fun way about them; I just want to be with her all the time. She is inside me; she is with me from head to toe even when she is fifteen miles away. For that matter, she could be on the other side of the world and I could feel her as if she were right beside me. I'm talking about her presence. It's all around me, everywhere I go.

I'm trying to take it slow with Alice but I'm busting at the seams with feelings that I want to put into words. The word 'love,' 'I love you Alice.' If I pour these words out of my mouth to soon I could scare her off. She might think I'm crazy. Nobody wants to marry a crazy person.

The only way I can describe this thing with Alice is that words are not necessary, touching physically is not necessary, my mind can say the word without my lips even moving and my body can feel Alice no matter where she is. This is the real thing. It's not a lustful thing that leads to darkness for me. My dad once asked me a question about Lucy, 'Are your lustful and loving desire the same, if so love will last the test of time, if you marry Lucy with only a lustful heart, your marriage will wither away. Your body is a treasure when love is in the picture; treat it as such. A mature love with sexuality is a gift to one another.' You see my dad knew long before I was aware that Lucy would never marry me because of my behavior. I refused to hear what he was trying to tell me.

Time to meet Alice is drawing near and now I'm waiting outside the restaurant in my car. I like to watch Alice walk; even though she is overweight, she has a certain movement of the hips that sends me.

Alice is now walking down the sidewalk toward the restaurant. She is wearing a sky blue dress belted with a wide white belt. Her sandals are white with just a slight heel, just enough to make her butt rise and stand out. Her purse is white leather with a shoulder strap and quite small in size. The white beads around her neck are big as marbles and hug her neck close. Her white earrings are round, but flat and match her beads around her neck. Alice takes off her sunglasses as she enters the restaurant.

I'm completely spellbound watching Alice walk. Only the closing of the restaurant door broke the trance. I quickly get out of the car, lock it, and take one last look at my hair in the side mirror to see if every hair is in place. I can feel that pop in my step as my excitement escalates. It's a good thing I'm young, for all this heart pounding excitement would put an old man in the grave.

As I enter the door, Alice is sitting at a table for two, facing the door. The look on her face as I walk through the door is sheer relief. My feelings are so strong for her that I wonder how she could even doubt that I would show.

Alice's elbow is resting on the table and she is giving a slight wave of the hand as if to say 'Hi, glad you could make it.' A slight grin came across her face, somewhat like the Mona Lisa smile. I just stood there for a while and my heart began beating on the wall of my chest like it was about to jump right out, I had to put my hand over it and say under my breath, 'heart be still.'

A moment later the hostess broke the spell by saying, "Would you like to be seated?" I pointed in the direction of Alice and said, "I'm with that lovely lady in the sky blue dress."

As I slowly descend into my chair, I study Alice's face, she begins to get a pink blush on her face and her eyes began shifting from left to right. She is showing a very shy side of herself that is so pure and heartwarming to me. My excitement rises because I do have an effect on her that she cannot hide. I break her moment with the words, "You look lovely tonight Alice."

Alice now locking her eyes on to mine responds, "You are very handsome yourself in your white shirt with a button down collar and silver cuff links. I'm so glad you could make it."

I said, "Perish the thought that I would miss any chance to be with you."

As we thumb through the menu, my eyes are once again drawn to Alice. Her skin is like peaches and cream. I can't help notice her low cut dress with her white breast showing just enough cleavage to make my heart once again begin to pound violently against my chest. I can't look at this menu, I can only look at Alice.

The moment is broken only as Alice said, "I eat here a lot and the French chop with a mushroom sauce is very tasty. On my salad, I like the traditional French dressing, seasoned oil and vinegar that is creamy and sweet with a pinkish color. I always get a long crusty loaf of French bread with the butter cooked on top. You can order whatever you want; I just didn't want you to think I would withhold information about the best dish on the menu. By the way, your wide cuff folded back and fastened with that silver cuff link is very French."

I said, "Thank you, it's nice that you notice the effort I put into dressing for this occasion. I appreciate your suggesting of what's best on the menu; I know it will be delicious."

Alice began reading the menu and it was in French. I didn't understand a word she was saying but her voice was eloquent. She glanced up from the menu to see if she has my undivided attention. I feel like I'm in a dream and I hope I never wake up. I could live my whole life with the feelings I have at this very moment.

Alice said, "I took French in college. It has a romantic tone like no other language on earth. I love knowing what all those words mean. I am no Julia Child but I am a pretty good cook myself. Someday I'll cook you a French meal at my house."

I said, "You just tell me when."

The waiter approached our table and Alice spoke French while placing our order. The waiter responded in French and I just sat there while they exchanged words and smiles. Not a single jealous feeling took over the moment to ruin the evening. I am actually enjoying watching her converse with the waiter. She is so in control.

Alice looked over the top of the menu and asked what kind of wine I liked; I replied that water is all I need. She cocked her head to the side as if she couldn't believe what she just heard.

When dinner arrived at our table, I dropped my head to give thanks to the Lord for this dinner and this wonderful day. Alice just watched in amazement.

Alice said, "I don't mean to scare you off but I'm agnostic, one who believes that there can be no proof of the existence of God but does not deny the possibility that God exists."

I responded, "Alice I have no problem with your belief system, this is a free country and religion is a very personal thing. I was raised in a very religious house but I was influenced by the 'me' generation. I was filled with narcissism, which made me less interested in other people, which in turn gave me an unrewarding life. My brother Jeff showed me the road to God. This is something my parents were never able to get thru to me. For me there is an unseen realm that is as real as the one we walk in. I have found it late in life but it will be in my entire future. I hope you can accept that about me."

Alice said, "I wouldn't change you for anything in this world. I'm so glad you are open and not hiding the real you. Who knows, you might be the one to convert me to religion."

The first bite of the French chop melted in my mouth. The flavor is bursting with richness of the sauce. Alice is watching my expression as I chew and she has a sly smile on her face knowing the joy of the flavors that are unique to anything I have ever tasted.

I said, "This is amazing, I don't even know how to describe what is in my mouth right now."

Alice said, "With French cooking it's all about the sauce."

I said, "Can you cook like this, you mentioned you cook French food?"

Alice said, "I have no plans to outsource cooking when I have a family, but this is something I cannot do, I've tried but just can't come close to this food. I will always visit this restaurant as long as they are in business."

I said, "You're not the only one. If you dump me, you may see me in this restaurant. You say the French make it all about the sauce, well I think you are a pretty saucy chick, the way you speak the language and introducing me to this amazing food. I could lick the sauce off this plate like I would do when I was a kid. I want every drop of this sauce."

Alice said, "I dare you, pick up that plate and clean it with a spit shine."

Well, I did pick the plate up and I cleaned it like I was ten years old. At first, I was a little embarrassed, and then I started giggling as if I was the one drinking wine. When I looked across the table at Alice, she was rolling with laughter with her wine glass in her hand. We are sharing memories at this table that will be with me for a lifetime. I've not experienced this much joy in a restaurant in my entire life.

Alice said, "Would you like to try the bread pudding? It's my favorite, and it has a great lemon sauce that you might like licking up."

I said, "I think you have impeccable taste when it comes to food."

Alice said, "They also have a great cheesecake with a raspberry sauce. I think I will order one of each and we can split them. That way we can have the best of both worlds."

Alice is spot on with the deserts; delicious is all I have to say about them. It's time for me to find out more about Alice, about what she expects out of life and how she plans to achieve it. I do not want to get in the way of any of her dreams. I want to live a charmed life with Alice.

I said, "Alice I want to know everything about you. I'm so intrigued by you."

Alice said, "What you see is what you get. Actually, I cannot believe we are sitting at this table together, God's gift to women, and me looking like a troll, a fat dwarf with a long nose. I do not know what is wrong with you, is it some deep psychological childhood problem? Excuse me, but when I drink wine, reality just slips off my tongue. I just throw up my feelings all over the place. I don't know when you will wake up from this weird trip you are on but I intend to have my fantasy world filled with you until the hallucination you are experiencing goes away."

I said, "I'm okay with you drinking a little wine, as long as you are in control, even God approves as in 1 Timothy 5:23, 'No longer drink only water, but use a little wine for the sake of your stomach and your frequent ailments,' and Psalms 104:14-15, 'Thou dost cause wine to gladden the heart of man.' I must say you seem very glad to be with me tonight. I hope it's not just the wine talking. I have a lot of faith in you and know you are very wise. Another quote from the Bible is Proverb 20:1, 'Wine is a mocker, strong drink a brawler; and whoever is led astray by it is not wise.' Alice, I will not let you be led astray. You are safe with me.

I want you to know that I have a very addictive personality so I'm cautious about drinking. The only thing I want to rule me is you. I want you to devour me and absorb me. I crossed the line of my boundaries when I lost control because of the intense feelings brought on by our physical touch. When I touch you, my mind begins to whirl. No woman has ever had this intense control over me. Normally I would never reveal my feelings this early into a relationship. I've broken all my boundaries when it comes to you Alice.

I never thought about the long-term consequences of having sex soon after meeting a woman until I met you Alice. Sex has taken a toll on me emotionally, and I ruined my early life because of lust without love. This is why I will wait until my wedding night to have my next sexual experience. For me, sex was a substitute for psychological intimacy. I refuse to make that kind of mistake ever again.

Ironically, beauty was the barometer in my hunt for a relationship, which always ended with sex talk and a fleeting feeling of passionate love. All these relationships left me in a crippling depression. I'm not on some weird trip that you seem to think I will suddenly snap out of, what I want is psychological intimacy that will last me for my lifetime. So if you think you will get to try me on and if I'm not a good sexual fit you can just dump me, you are wrong."

Alice said, "Let me clarify my thinking, are you saying I'm not going to get to sleep with you unless I marry you?"

I said, "That's right."

Alice said, "I feel a lot safer now. Looks like all I have to protect is my heart. I appreciate your frankness along with your flattery of the effect I seem to have on you.

I'm fully aware that physical attractiveness is a desirable quality, and that it's not what keeps a couple together. You must love what is inside of a person, but I cannot help seeing how gorgeous you are sitting there across the table from me.

The thrills of lust are addicting, and every time I fall in lust, I lose my mind. I have a tendency to self-destruct from the magical mystical feelings lust creates.

All my lust relationships had a natural end; the road just ran out, it was time to move on. For me unexplained melancholy comes with lust. My moods bounce up and down like a yo-yo on a string. I worry so much about the relationship ending, that I actually cause it to end."

I said, "Alice, I know just what you are talking about. I see all men trying to steal my girl. I'm always on guard and in a state of constant tension. I believe by worrying I'm keeping our relationship safe from someone stealing her from me. I worry about this all the time. When I try not to worry, I become anxious and out of control. By keeping my girlfriends away from other people, I feel safe that she will not leave me for another man. I thought that by worrying, I could avoid worse things from happening; well I was wrong. They all left me."

Alice said, "Looks like we have a lot in common. Not the best traits to have, but at least we will be able to understand how the other feels. That should help us avoid problems.

I'm on cloud nine right now and you are fully aware of the situation. You know the impact you are having on me, I can tell. I'm going to roll with it and hope you don't destroy me in this heavenly moment. Even though I don't know if heaven exists or not, if it does, it will feel like I do at this place and time. I could stay like this forever."

Alice may have had too much wine; she is gazing off like she is in another world. Alice has opened my eyes to the fact that joy is being happy with what we have rather than what we don't have. Just knowing that I have an effect on Alice, that sends her into another world, brings me joy. Living in this moment where Alice is bearing her soul to me is a miraculous breakthrough to my future wife.

Now that I'm at peace with God, I can find fulfillment on earth with Alice by my side. He has brought her to me even though she does not know Him.

Alice flashed her marvelously illuminating smile in my direction as she took another sip of wine. I watched her mouth with precise visualization and without restraint, I imaged my mouth being that wine glass and Alice tasting my lips.

The silence we are experiencing is so intense neither of us is able to break it. Her tantalizing lips are puffy with color from the red wine. She presses her lips together as if she is reading my mind.

The waiter approached our table and asked, "Is there anything else I can bring you?"

Alice and the waiter had a conversation in French and the waiter gave me a smile, handed me a check, then handed Alice a check.

With any other woman, I would be upset that she had a conversation with the waiter, but Alice was so poised and eloquent that all I felt was pleased to watch her converse in French.

My soul has finally found peace. My soul is the most important thing in my life; it is what I take with me when I leave this world. Alice is food for my soul. Without someone to love, life has no value. Alice has brought value to my life that I have never experienced.

We each place our money on our tickets for the waiter to pick up. Alice has a half-full glass of wine and tells the waiter thanks for the good job he has done as he begins counting the money. She tells him the extra is his tip for being so attentive. He gives a nod of appreciation as he leaves the table.

Alice said, "There is something I have to tell you. When I talked about being in lust before, what I meant was, I thought I was in love. I'm actually in love with life itself. It doesn't take much to get me overflowing with joy, and to me joy is love. What I'm trying to say is that I'm able to love someone without making love to them. In other words, I'm still a virgin."

I said, "Somehow I knew that. Don't ask me how I knew it, because I could never explain it, I just know. You see, God made you just for me. I only wish I were also a virgin that way I could be as special to you as you are to me."

Alice said, "One of us needs to know what to do, that is if this fantasy of yours lasts that long. I really must be going; I have an early appointment in the morning."

I think Alice embarrassed herself. Her white skin is turning bright red. It was as if the word virgin jumped out of her mouth and spilled all over the table and made a big mess. She did not mean to tell me how inexperienced she really is. All I can think is how special our wedding night will be.

Alice is walking fast out the door. I'm right behind her and as she clears the door, I grab her hand and turn her around and kiss her on her lips. It is just a peck but very powerful. As our lips parted, I could still feel her lips on mine. It is a tingling feeling with a fullness of joy that fills my entire body.

I said, "Alice I just wanted to say I couldn't be happier that you are a virgin. Can't you see how perfect things are for us? It's as if we have been sprinkled with all the fine gifts that life has to offer. We have this intense feeling for each other topped with your innocence, there is not a gift on earth that could mean more to me on our wedding night. Be proud of your strength to resist the power of the flesh, which you saved for your wedding night. The sweetness we will share on that night will make it all worth waiting for. I will hold you tight that night so your body won't explode from all the joy I will bring you. We will share in a love that encompasses both physical and emotional joy that will drive us to near hysteria. I want you to lose all control and melt into my arms. Alice, I love you with an extraordinary love, will you marry me?"

Alice said, "Ed, this is like a dream, I'm dizzy with all your words running around in my head, and that peck you gave me on my lips is stronger than any feeling I've had in my entire life, but you see I'm afraid. If you wake up from whatever is going on in your head, you will destroy me. I will never be able to just bounce back from all this. I will be buried alive in regret and feelings of loss if I were to lose you. This thing we have is stronger than I knew was possible. We have to slow it down or I'm going to go off the deep end. I'm not as strong as you are and I know it. You just don't know what you are doing to me."

I said, "Alice, you are so safe with me, I would die before I would ever hurt you."

Alice said, "You better not, that is, you better not die on me."

I said, "You make me feel like I will live forever. You give my body strength and energy, and I feel like I will fly into heaven with you by my side."

Alice said, "You better. I really have to go now, I had a lovely evening, and I will give you an answer when I'm sure, this is all going so fast. I have to pinch myself now and then to make sure I'm not just dreaming."

Alice left me standing there with my mouth open, unable to say a word. It's as if my legs are paralyzed, helpless and unable to move. I just poured my heart out to the woman I love and she is afraid of my love.

Chapter 4
Slowing it Down

Alice has a point. If a woman came on to me so fast, I would be leery, suspicious, and distrustful myself. I'm going to have to get a hold on my feelings and control what I say. I want Alice for the rest of my life and I don't need to blow it because I want her to know what is in my heart, all the time.

Alice knows now that I want to make her my wife and now it is up to her to make the next bold move. I intend to continue my pursuit of happiness only in a more normal way. I must exhibit a little control. I shall be more sensitive in my romantic approach to Alice.

My parents always told me that our character determines our behavior; I understand what they were talking about now. I love Alice like nothing I've ever experienced in my lifetime. My behavior may seem somewhat odd, but my character cannot be questioned. I will love and protect Alice her entire life, I will always be the one thing she can count on, forever.

I understand why Alice would question my character because I was a drug addict for many years. If I were her, this would definitely be a red flag raised against my character. Alice is smart enough to know that you don't jump into a relationship just because it feels good to be around someone, you could get stuck in a nightmare. It happens every day to some poor soul who thought it felt right to be with a certain person only to learn later that they were hooking up with the Devil himself. You can get totally blinded by strong feelings and become unable to even see what's down the road.

I have a friend who married a woman because he had strong feelings for her and thought that was all that mattered. His life and marriage became his nightmare.

My friends name is Doug and we were friends from school since the first grade. He lived only two blocks from me so we road bikes and hung out in the neighborhood the whole time we were growing up. Doug is one of the good guys who married out of lust without even considering the character of the woman who he gave his heart to.

Doug's wife's name is Molly and I've never known a more self-centered individual in my entire life. Molly is beautiful on the outside but a monster on the inside. Everything in their life had to center around Molly or she would become violent. The longer they were married the more frequent the outburst of rage became. Once she hit Doug with a five-pound barbell that caused him great injury to his face, just because he refused to give her money to get her nails done professionally by a nail technician. At the time, they were struggling to make ends meet. Doug was working and going to college. Molly was a stay at home mom with two children. Because money or lack of money was a real issue at the time in the marriage, Doug offered to buy the nail polish and do Molly's nails himself. Molly took this as an insult and broke Doug's nose with the barbell. The trip to the doctor's office cost more than the nail technician would in a year. Molly's response to the situation was, "Oh you can go to the doctor to get your nose fixed but I can't get my nails done."

As time went on with many battles in-between, Doug graduated from college and landed a great job with an oil company as a geologist. Molly continued to be a stay at home mom and the kids were starting to go to school. One boy was in the first grade and the other boy was in pre-school.

Boys have a tendency to play rough with each other and these two boys always seemed to have bruises on their bodies. At one of the parent teacher meetings, Doug and Molly were asked about the bruises. Molly became very defensive and began calling the teacher who inquired about the bruises offensive names. This behavior raised a red flag, and the state was called in to investigate the situation.

Molly had her fight or flight trigger pulled and she gathered her children up the next morning and left the house claiming Doug was harming her children. She went to a women's shelter, got a lawyer, filed for a divorce, and claimed Doug was battering her and the children. She panicked because she thought the state would take her children from her and Doug. She knew if she acted first, Doug would have to prove his innocence in court.

In court, Doug was made to pay child support, and alimony, court-ordered allowance for support, due to legal separation.

Doug was ordered by the court to attend classes on anger management and parenting. The classes had to be sponsored by the state and it was four months before an opening was available and the classes took twelve months to complete. That meant Doug could not even visit his children for a year and four months. This is lost time with his children he will never get back.

Even though Doug was not allowed around his children for over a year, bruises were still showing up on the children. The children claimed the bruises came from the two of them fighting. Could this be where the bruises were coming from all along, or could it be that Molly was abusive to her children just like she was to Doug? Could she be coaching the children on what to say? Only the children know for sure what happened in that house.

The courts eventually gave Doug joint custody, and alimony and child support stopped for Molly. The whole thing winded up being a two-year nightmare for Doug and his children. I would say Molly was lacking good character and Doug paid the price for not taking the time to know what Molly was really like. You can only hide the real you for so long. Molly ruined her husband's life and caused her children a tremendous amount of pain by not being able to see their dad. She destroyed their family.

Doug married Molly only three months after meeting her. Doug did not check out Molly's family or even Molly for that matter. As Doug got to know Molly's family he became aware that Molly's parents were divorced. Molly's mother put her dad through the same scenario. Molly learned her behavior from her mother. Their characters were undesirable when it comes to family values. Hopefully, Molly will become a better person some day. Doug does everything in his power to help Molly become a better person at a distance.

Molly wanted to get back with Doug to make the family whole, but Doug fell out of love with Molly and it would not be fair to the family to marry someone you didn't love.

Doug learned a lesson the hard way. His life was turned upside down and his children were victims of their parent's abuse. Part of the abuse was Doug's fault because he didn't take the time to know what Molly was really like. It is your responsibility to know the mother of your children before you create them.

My mom always told me that when a person is put in a pinch, they resort to what they learned as a child. This is why it is so important that you get to know the person you love really well before you marry them.

Doug told me he forgave Molly for destroying the family so he could move on with his life. You just can't live the good life with pent-up bitter feelings in your heart.

Doug and Molly were adults and adults are responsible for their actions. The true victims in all this mess is the children. They live in two homes that lack the true meaning of the family unit.

I've learned a lot just by observing what happened to my best friend and would never let lust be the driving force when I start my family. Alice is the first woman I've ever asked to marry me. Lucy was beautiful, and I was spellbound by that beauty, and tried to change her into what I wanted in a woman, but that never works. You have to accept people for who they are. That's who they become when they get into a pinch. I nearly destroyed myself trying to change Lucy into what I wanted her to be. She is so beautiful I couldn't get her out of my mind. I wanted her to act the way I wanted her to be. I wanted to steal her identity.

I've learned my lesson in life but luckily, I was the only casualty in the relationship. No children were involved and Lucy went on with her life. It was as if I had no real effect on Lucy, she was just glad to get rid of me. She continues to live her self-consumed life with shallow relationships. She even got married a couple of times. I kept tabs on her until I met Alice. Now Lucy is in my past forever. Suddenly Lucy just didn't matter anymore. I never knew I could just turn Lucy off in my mind until I met Alice. I thought Lucy would haunt me my entire life.

Alice is on my mind non-stop, but I'm desperately trying to keep it light instead of intense. I need to give Alice all the room she wants in this relationship. It's like I'm with her even though she is no where around, I can feel her presence.

It's been two days since I've seen Alice or talked to her. I'm not letting this drive me crazy or anything like that, but I'm starting to miss Alice. She has my cell number and I keep the phone charged and with me at all times. I wouldn't take a chance on missing a call from Alice.

I think it would be nice to have lunch today at the fast food restaurant where I first met Alice. Maybe she will be there.

I arrive at the exact time when I first saw Alice, knowing this is her lunch hour. As I enter the restaurant, I scan the room hoping for a glance of Alice in the line or at a table. She is not in the restaurant. I order my lunch, grab a table and visually image the first time I met Alice. My imagination is so strong I can feel Alice in the line of people I'm looking at even though she is not there. Joy is filling all my senses and I can see Alice walking to my table, as she sits down I can smell the perfume and see her shinny white teeth as she smiles at me. I reach across the table to touch her and she vanishes. How can it be possible that I can feel her presence so strongly and yet Alice is not physically sitting across the table from me?

As I come to my senses, the most beautiful creature asks if she can share my table. The chair across from me is the only empty chair in the room. I nod my head giving the okay. I'm just being sociable. How could I possible turn this lovely creature down and make her eat in her car, or stand in the corner. She places her tray on the table, pulls the chair out, smoothes her dress against the back of her legs and sits down. She says, 'Thank you'. I cannot help but admire the beauty God has blessed upon this woman. Her long blond hair falls off her shoulder with soft curls. Her eyes are as green as poison, and her skin is an olive color with a lovely sheen. We sit across from each other in total silence. Occasionally she glances up and smiles at me, I return the gesture.

As I glance out the window, I see Alice walking to the door. I nod at the beautiful creature across from me, grab my tray and head for the door. Just as I clear my tray, Alice opens the door.

I said, "Hello Alice"

Alice said, "Hi, I see you just finished your lunch. Are you leaving?"

I said, "Can I sit with you while you eat? I promise to keep a cool head and not make you uncomfortable."

Alice said, "Sure."

As Alice placed her order, I glanced back at the beautiful creature with whom I shared my table and she winked at me. I quickly turned around and kept my eyes on Alice.

With tray in hand, Alice walks over to the condiment bar and gathers packages of seasoning for her food. As Alice turns, the beautiful woman with whom I just shared a table with waved us over. It was like a hot coal rushed through my entire body. Alice started walking in the direction of the beautiful creature and my breathing became labored. I could feel sweat popping up on my forehead. I continued to follow behind Alice and all the time fear was building, that this beautiful creature who I don't even know may say something to Alice and ruin everything.

As Alice approached the table, the beautiful creature leaned back so she could see me, and said, "I would like to return the favor, I'm just finishing up my meal and you two can have this table."

As the beautiful creature walked out the door, Alice looked at me and said, "What was all that about, do you two know each other?"

I said, "I've never seen her before today. She had the same situation we just had, every table was full and she asked if she could share my table. I couldn't tell her no."

Alice said, "And it's just a coincidence, a seemingly planned sequence of accidentally occurring events, that she just also happens to be drop dead gorgeous."

I said, "Alice I could have kept the truth from you and just not told you that I didn't have a clue what she was talking about, but I never want to lie to you. Even if the situation is painful for me to talk about, I will never lie to you, we will just work our way through the tough times."

Alice said, "Just what brings you back to the very spot where we first met? You haven't called me in days. You pour your heart out, and then you ignore me. I find this to be very strange behavior. I would say you are stalking me, but when we met, you were already in this restaurant. Or I could say, this is the restaurant where you meet all your chicks, and it looks like I'm trying to find you."

I said, "It doesn't matter, we are here together and for me that is all that matters. I want a normal relationship with you Alice, and whatever it takes, I'm willing to do. I'm just trying to slow it down like you asked. I don't want to scare you off. I want you to be comfortable with me always."

Alice said, "I will never be comfortable with gorgeous chicks making eyes at you. You will just have to accept my insecurities."

I said, "I completely understand why you would question the situation and I'm glad that you do, if you held it in you would always be wondering about the situation. Because you confront me, we are able to get to the root of the problem, pull it out of our garden of paradise, and get rid of it. I was never able to share my insecurities with Lucy and lied about problems all the time. Nothing ever got fixed. You see Alice, it is healthy to air your feelings and find out there was nothing to worry about.

I had to learn these things when I was in therapy to get my mind right so I could get off my addiction to drugs. I thought by worrying and isolating my girlfriends, I could keep my jealousy under control and that isolation was the solution to my problems.

Alice I think this is a teachable moment. My personal opinion is that jealousy is caused from a flawed gene. You can't just make it go away, it is part of you, but you can control it and not let it ruin your life. The one thing you truly own in this world is your life, take care of it. Keep your jealousy in check and don't let others exploit your weakness. When they spot it, they like to have fun with it.

There is a bit of wisdom in the Bible that I always remind myself of in Proverbs 27:6, "The wounds inflicted by a friend are more precious than the flattery of an enemy." It is the enemy who tries to make you jealous.

I ask myself, "Would you be so rude as to not answer the door for God when He knocked on it? Remember that He knocks on your door every day. God is my best friend and He helps me with my jealous heart. God literally seems like a comic-book hero to me. Now that I know God in a very personal and intimate way, he blocks my jealous thoughts. I put my life in God's hands and He gives me strength to fight my weakness."

Alice said, "Well, I'm glad for you having someone to stop the pain caused from a jealous heart, because you are so good looking it is much easier for you to deal with than it is for me, looking like I do. My looks make me very insecure; they are the icing on my cake of jealousy. I can't help it. If you weren't so good looking we wouldn't be having this problem."

I said, "Please make room for me in your life, I could go to a plastic surgeon and ask him to ugly me up a little."

Alice said, "You better not. Let's just work on my warped mind. If you were able to get past the mental flaw of jealousy with your God, maybe you could ask Him to help me. The brain is really something special, we have the power to change it, if we want. I won't lie to you Ed, when that woman winked at you as she left the table, I could have pulled every hair out of her head."

I said, "I have very recently learned about the minds of women. A chemical happens when attraction is the base of the relationship. You get all wet because of the attraction. It is a physical thing that you have no control over. It makes women more aggressive. However you don't have to act on it. I understand the gift of sexuality; I'm looking for something much deeper than that. I want the inner serenity, the essence of life, that what is inside of me, love. I have mastered the art of delayed gratification, beautiful women no longer own me, I've fallen out of sync with them. I've suffered the ravages of physical and emotional abuse that attraction to the wrong person can bring, I'm ready for the real thing.

I think our connection and friendship will last a lifetime because of your warm, enthusiastic and funny nature. You are able to pour your heart all over me and I love bathing in it.

It's worth it to me to risk rejection from you even if it's just because you want to protect your heart. I don't know how to make it any plainer to you, that your heart is safe with me. I will never intentionally cause you emotional pain. I had a shower of anxious thoughts when you asked me to slow it down, I thought you wanted to get rid of me; I was mortified. You have that effect on me, lasting repercussions that I may never recover from. You see Alice, this is a two way street. You could ruin me. Now that I've given you all my heart I will never take it away. For me, you radiate the joy for life with your vibrant smile. I don't want to become a prisoner of your past; I want to share your future. You need to learn more about women in order to understand why they want to cause problems in other people's life. If that woman could break us up she could move in. A good person would never have said a word. That woman was trying to cause trouble in our relationship."

Alice said, "This is like a fairy tale for me. It just doesn't seem true. I could let my feelings take over and put my mind on a shelf and see what happens, but that's not me. I never put myself in a dangerous situation. I can experience you without going all gaga over you. If you can accept that part of me, we might have a future."

I said, "Alice, I accept you any way you want me to. I just hope you don't mind if I go all gaga over you. I want to experience what it's like to just let it all go. Not hold anything back. Free my mind and body, to drink you up like a cool glass of lemonade on a hot day. The bitter and the sweet all mixed up that refreshes the body. That is all that I want from you Alice."

Things got quiet and Alice started eating her lunch. I gazed out the window as my heart bubbled with joy knowing Alice will take a chance on me. I'm putting her in the driver's seat with our relationship. If Alice has control of where our relationship is headed, she might lighten up and have fun with it. Love should be fun, free from anxiety, uneasiness, and distress about future uncertainties. Love should be the ultimate freedom and security should be the foundation it sits on, freedom from doubt, or fear of a broken heart. This is what I have to give to Alice. All Alice has to do is take it.

Alice said, "You know Ed, when you say that all you want from me is the bitter and the sweet, in reality you are asking for all of me. That's a lot.

Time will tell if I'm able to hold your interest or not. I'm in no hurry like you seem to be, so you must understand and be willing to take it slow.

I think we should meet each other's friends and see how we fit in. My best friend Sofia and her husband Joe are dying to meet you. Are you available this Saturday around 7:00 p.m.?"

I said, "Alice, I'm available anytime you want to be with me. All you have to do is ask."

Alice said, "Great, here is the address, I will meet you there. They are already expecting me, I'm bringing a bottle of wine, and Sofia really likes flowers, if you would like to bring a rose for the table she would be overjoyed."

I said, "I will bring a red rose and I'm excited about

meeting your friends. I'm more excited about seeing you Saturday and spending time with you even if I have to share you with your friends. I won't have any trouble finding this house; it's close to where I go to church."

Alice said, "Great, I hope you like them. I've known Sofia since we were in the first grade. She is more like a sister than a friend. Her husband is a good guy, I know you will like him.

I came in here for a light lunch and winded up in a very heavy conversation. I'm glad you were here. I needed to see you and talk to you. I'm excited about Saturday. I hope you like my friends."

I just melted when Alice said she was glad I was here. It was like music to my ears. My heart is busting at the seams.

Chapter 5
Sofia and Joe

As I shower, thoughts of Alice fill my head. I'm high as a kite just thinking about seeing her and now she wants me to meet her friends. That is progress. Friends are precious gifts and just the thought of sharing Alice's friends with her tonight tells me she is mine.

A jingle pops in my mind as I lather up:
My sweet Alice
I wish you no malice
My sweet Alice
I want to build you a palace
Just west of Dallas
My sweet Alice

This is what Alice does for me. She energizes my mind and body. I get up early in the mornings without even setting an alarm. The first thing I think about is Alice and I'm excited about the day because Alice is in my heart and mind.

I never even thought about lyrics to a song. They just jump into my head out of nowhere. This is what she does to me. It's amazing.

As I comb my hair, I think about the red rose I'm to purchase for Sofia. I want it to be the most luxurious, most expensive variety of any red rose she has ever seen and I plan to purchase its twin for Alice. That's right, two red roses, only the best for my Alice.

As I knock on the door, my heart begins to race. Alice's friends do very well for themselves. They live in a very nice neighborhood with manicured grounds and trees that must be over a hundred years old. Their house is large enough to accommodate a family of ten. I'm guessing at least four bathrooms.

Alice answers the door, her hair is arranged in soft curls on top of her head, it gives me chills as Alice eloquently takes my hand and guides me into the house of her friends. As she introduces me to Sofia and Joe, my eyes are locked on her lips. Out of the corner of my eye, I see Joe reaching his hand out, and the spell is broken as I shake his hand and say, "Nice to meet you Joe, and Sofia I'm honored to meet someone who has been Alice's friend since the first grade."

Everyone chuckled at that comment, and I hand Alice the first rose, and then kiss her on the end of her nose. Alice turns as red as the rose I handed her. She doesn't like her nose, but to me it's the most beautiful nose in the whole world. Then I hand Sofia her rose and she puts it to her nose and rolls her eyes as if it smells delicious to her. Sofia picks up a vase from the counter, fills it half full of water and puts her rose in it. Alice smells her rose, touches its perfect petals and places it into the vase. Sofia places the vase in the center of the dinner table between two candles, and then we all go into the living room and chat for a while.

Alice, Sofia and Joe all have a glass of wine and I have my standard glass of water with a slice of lemon. There is a lot of small talk about the weather, news of the day and then sports. The ladies leave the room to prepare dinner and Joe proceeds to tell me about his favorite teams. Joe is very knowledgeable about sports and we shared stories about famous players and the moves they made.

Sofia said, "I hate to break up this male comradeship, but we wouldn't want our leg of lamb to get cold, now would we?"

As I sat down at the table, I asked if I could give thanks to God for the food we were about to receive. Sofia nodded her head, as if to say yes, I gave thanks for the food and work Sofia did preparing this feast. Everyone bowed their heads in respect for my words.

The leg of lamb melts in my mouth. The taste of bay leaves is strong and makes the lamb flavoring perfect. Sofia is an outstanding cook, I compliment her on the leg of lamb and she informed me the recipe has been in her family for over one hundred years.

Joe began telling me about how he met Sofia at a football game and that it was love at first sight. They have been together ever since. Joe talked about his career of homebuilding, but lives in a fifty-year-old house. Joe explained the richness of the Two-hundred-year-old oak trees in the yard, and how the houses were built so much better fifty years ago. They used 2x6 boards then and now only use 2x4 boards. The old houses are just built stronger. As Joe finished talking about himself, he said, "Tell me about yourself, Ed."

I said, "I'm a late bloomer. Right now, I work for an oil company and go to school at night to become a doctor. I'm training in pain management and addiction to medicine. Alice knows the problems I've had with addiction; she also knows that addiction is in my past."

Joe said, "We have no secrets at this table, Alice has shared your past with us and we are looking forward to your present with Alice. Nobody knows about the future, we just kind of make it as we go. Right now Alice is crazy about you, and Sofia and I are not judgmental of anyone but ourselves. Today you and Alice are a couple and we wish both of you all the joy you can stand.

Ed, I've never talked to anyone about addiction, if you wouldn't mind telling me more about your addiction, I'm all ears."

I said, "Everyone has their own story of why they became an addict. Through counseling, I found my addiction stemmed from my childhood. You see I was a very cute kid. I've been told I'm adorable now and adorable when I was born. This is how my mother sees me. I could do no wrong in her eyes. Everything I did was cute, and discipline was not part of my parent's vocabulary while I was growing up. Well, it's not cute anymore. I've lost a lot of years to bad behavior.

You see, I thought all the girls I dated should treat me as my parents did, like I could do no wrong. Everything had to revolve around my needs. When it didn't I would try to control the girls by isolating them from the world. When they rejected this behavior, instead of lightning up, I became more intense with the behavior. They all left me and I was unable to deal with the pain. I turned to drugs to numb the rejection.

My parents never meant to hurt me and to this day, I've never told them they were the root cause of my addiction problem. I just can't see how hurting them late in life would benefit anyone. I've discussed this with Jeff, my brother, and he promised me he would never tell them anything about what we discussed. I trust him with my life; he would never try to put distance between my parents and me. Jeff knows that it should come out of my mouth, not his, if they are ever told. Jeff would not betray me for anything in the world and that is why he is my sounding board. You have to have someone to share your thoughts with. That helps with the healing.

By understanding why I became an addict I was able to break the cycle. I know how to deal with my disease only because I was able to get to the root cause.

I was very fortunate that I wasn't incarcerated, I just never got caught. I'm an exception to the rule of why people become drug addicts, most have mental disorders and are trying to self-medicate, others have learning disabilities, when you are different and you feel uncomfortable you are likely to become stressed, and drugs and alcohol cover your stresses.

If I can help people deal with the disease of addiction by the recognition of why they become drug addicts in the first place, I will be a success in life. I want to work with teenagers; that is when most addicts are created.

At one time only 10% of people were addicts. That number is on the rise due to drugs that make a person an addict only after using a few times. It is a problem that will plague all of us if we don't try to put the brakes on.

I'm talking about an epidemic. You see if a mother is using certain drugs while she is pregnant, she can damage her baby's nervous system and it can be permanent. There are children right now who have to be medicated ten times a day just to calm them down because the mother was using methamphetamines while pregnant. I want to prevent this from happening to as many young people as possible.

If the mother damages her baby's nervous system, that baby is more likely to become addicted to drugs when they become teenagers just because they start self medicating. They are looking for something to stop the pain of their nervous disorder, something that is stronger than a doctor prescribes.

What I have learned in my studies of addiction medicine is that every addict has a reason why they become addicts. We must first find the reason, and then treat the addiction.

Being an addict took the joy out of my life. My mother always told me that in the word joy the 'j' stood for Jesus, the 'o' stood for others and the 'y' stood for yourself, in that order. I had things out of order. It was all about me. I lived in sin, and the middle letter in sin is 'I'.

Now that my mind is clear from drugs, joy is in my

life once again, all because I have control of my illness called addiction. Once I asked myself, 'Why do I need drugs?', I realized it was because I was only concerned about myself. The price of my vice is just too much. My vice was stealing my life. I just have an addictive personality. It was fed with drugs at one time but that is all behind me now.

Alice is my addiction, whether she accepts my disease or not is up to her. I feel deeply for Alice and it is a gift I hope she accepts. I can't imagine life without her.

Joe is that a good enough explanation of what it's like to be a drug addict?"

As I looked up into Joe's eyes, a shudder ran through by body, much like when the wind ripples the leaves of a tree. In Joe's eyes, I could see the suffocating realness of human wretchedness.

Joe said, "You can't make Alice responsible for your happiness. You are asking too much of her. If she can't feed your new addiction to her spirit you could ruin her life with your disappointment.

When we fail at love, we all become helpless and depressed at least momentarily. Most can pick themselves up, shrug their shoulders, and start all over again. Alice is not like most people, she feels deeper. She loves with her brain. The brain and the immune system are connected, not through nerves but through hormones, the chemical messengers that drift through the blood and can transmit emotional state from one part of the body to another. If you decided Alice wasn't the one for your love addiction, you could ruin her mind forever.

Ed, you are very handsome, movie star material, I know women are attracted to you, beautiful women, the kind that would be hard to ignore. Is this the kind of life you are offering Alice, a life of competing with beautiful women for your attention?"

I said, "First of all, Alice is not responsible for my

happiness, only I can control my happiness. Second, I will never destroy Alice's mind; it is my treasure chest. Third, beautiful women are self-consumed, spoiled and just not right for me. I can't help it if they look at me.

What you must understand Joe, is that I love Alice like no person I've ever loved in my life. I will protect that love from any harm. I promise you Alice will have happiness like she has never known, and for her entire life. This love of mine for her will last the test of time. I will love her even from the grave.

Life is all about special moments, when I saw Alice, it was the moment that changed my life. Looking deeply into her eyes, the day we met, I could see our entire future. It was deep love that cannot be rooted out. Alice feels the same way I do. This is a two way street. Just ask her."

Joe said, "Alice, would you like to comment on what Ed has told us?"

Alice said, "It's like a dream that I'm afraid I might wake up from. Look at him, prince charming himself. When I touch just his hand, my body can feel him from head to toe. It's amazing and frightening at the same time. If he were to change his mind after we are intimate, it could ruin my life forever. Losing him is a frightening thought for me.

I'm not real strong minded, I hurt easily. I don't put myself out there to get hurt as a general rule so I don't have to deal with the pain of loss. If Ed wanted to, he could cause me the kind of pain that I may not be able to recover from. I'm telling you this Ed so you know what you are getting yourself into.

I can create joy with just what I think might be happening. An example of my ability to create joy is when I thought a brown thrasher bird was hiding in a bush. The brown thrasher is a North American bird, with a dark-streaked breast and reddish-brown back. They are very shy by nature and seldom seen. This particular day that I spotted a brown thrasher in the green thick bushes, joy and excitement filled my body as I gazed upon the lovely creature. Slowly I stepped closer, so not to startle the brown thrasher, and get a closer look at it. With each step, the joy and excitement would build until I felt like I was busting at the seams, when suddenly I was close enough to see it was a brown and reddish leaf and not a brown thrasher. You would think someone stabbed me in the heart with a spear. All the wonderful feelings that just moments earlier filled my body, vanished with the reality of what I was looking at, a leaf."

I said, "Alice if you will let me be your brown thrasher I promise never to be a leaf. Your joy for life is safe with me, I promise."

Sofia said, "My dear Alice, I say go for it. I'm a good judge of character, you know that about me. I like Ed, and more than that, I like the way he feels about you. Don't let him get away Alice, take a chance on love, after all you're not getting any younger."

I feel threatened by Joe, and welcomed with open arms by Sofia. Men think different then women, Joe is just looking out for Alice. I respect his feelings of wanting to protect Alice, but faulting me because of the way I look, he will just have to get over that. I will prove to him that I will never hurt Alice.

Alice said, "We need to lighten things up around here. All this drama has made me hungry for cheesecake. I made a New York style cheesecake with strawberries on top. I used real cheese and cream so it will be very rich in flavor. Raise your hand if you would like a piece."

Everyone raised their hands and Alice served the cheesecake. I see my future of putting on twenty pounds if Alice cooks like this all the time. No wonder she is a little fleshy.

The conversation lightened up with desert and Joe began telling funny stories about the way he was raised.

Joe's parents had a dairy farm and Joe always had a cow utter in his hand. The cows were always glad to see Joe and his bucket because their utters would be full and uncomfortable, and Joe provided relief.

Joe said, "I would always have my fresh milk early in the morning, I would squeeze the utter, point it at my mouth and drink up. Some would miss my mouth and hit my face, that is why my complexion is like peaches and cream, really fresh milk. After filling my buckets, I would skim the cream off and make half of the cream into butter by churning it with a butter churn. The other half was sold as cream and much of it made wonderful cheesecake like we are eating right now.

As we made money with the milk cows, my father purchased automatic milking machines. My job became easier. No more milk drank straight from the utter."

I like Joe, he is down to earth and he cares about Alice's heart. I'm glad she has friends that care about her welfare.

Sofia said, "Coffee anyone?"

Everyone raised their hand but me. I'm still just drinking water. The only stimulate I need is Alice. Every time I just look at her, I get all the energy I need. As we leave the dinner table, Alice touches her rose and then smells the center. She glances at me and a smile spreads across her face. Our eyes lock and suddenly I'm as light as a feather. This is the effect she has on me.

I said, "Alice, you are lovely tonight, pretty as that rose you are smelling right now."

Alice said, "I wish I was as perfect as this red rose, not a blemish on it and the petals look like velvet. Its fragrance has an aroma that only nature can provide, an intangible quality that cannot be put in a bottle for perfume. Just looking at it gives me a merry heart."

I said, "Alice, there is an old saying, 'A merry heart doeth good like medicine.' You can call me Dr. Ed if you like. Any time you need a rose, just call me."

Alice said, "Everyone, I believe Ed has reached the borders of sanity. He genuinely had reached a catatonic state of love resulting in very strange behavior. He has reached an obsessive intense desire to be with me. In his infatuation, he aspires to be the love doctor. Being sober has taken sanity to a whole new level. Maybe I should lay off the wine for a while."

Alice is having fun with me and I love it. My thirst is quenched by her eloquent appeal for good humor. She sees me to the depths of my soul; she sees that I have transformed my mind and heart into the desire for a lasting relationship with a family, and home, to give me extraordinary purpose, peace and joy. Family is the lasting mental gyration resulting in a utopian existence, which we should all strive for.

My banquet of senses are lost in a physical sensation which are the result of Alice, who is the love of my life, full of sweet nectar like the rose she smells. The intensity of my love for Alice is becoming greater than I can bear. Suddenly, my mouth is on hers, I've lost all control. It is only a peck, but stronger than any kiss I have experienced in my twenty-seven years on earth. No longer will I go through life in mediocrity, I have Alice.

Chapter 6
Spending time with Friends and Family

As I wake to the sound of Jeff stirring in the kitchen, thoughts of Alice's lips on mine the night before ring out the words, 'true intimacy.' It is a physical sensation, as strong as the act of lovemaking, yet only a peck on the mouth. Ah, Alice you are really something.

Last night I had the time of my life. Joe and Sofia are good people, full of personality. I will fit right in. Making me talk about my lost years in addiction makes it where I now have nothing to hide. Joe made me put it all out on the table; no secrets with Joe and Sofia, they are like family. Let's get the dirty laundry clean. Air it out.

My brother Jeff, God's angel for me, took away my self-destruct button, and made my new life possible. Jeff also made me aware that a bad relationship is not better than being alone with no relationship. Time by yourself can be rewarding if you make it a good time.

Jeff made me able to say no to a self love, and just enjoy myself in a fuller way. Life has a deeper meaning than self-gratification. Jeff helps keep my life in check.

I spent five whole years without even a date. I cleaned up my life, left my addiction to drugs and beautiful women in the dust. Soul searching is all I did for those years. I put my life back together with a goal of making a family and providing for them with a career that would make the need for money not a factor. I'm not saying that money is a cure-all, life will always throw you a curve ball now and then, what I'm saying is, money makes life easier. I just want my future to be the best possible one I can provide.

Jeff said, "Good morning Ed, the smell of bacon must have got you out of that bed. You got in late last night; you woke me when you closed the door. Did you like Alice's friends?"

I said, "I fit in like a glove. I had the time of my life. How lucky can a man get when the love of his life has cool friends to top everything off with. I'm telling you little brother, God has stepped into my life and everything is coming up roses."

Jeff said, "That's great, friends are important in life. I'm sure you will build many beautiful memories with them.

I thought you might like to know that Chelsea Songbird is on her way to town and she is coming over tonight for supper, would you like to invite Alice?"

I said, "Sounds like a great idea, I'll call her right after I fill my belly. You both are responsible for the man I am today. Alice will be grateful to spend time with the two of you. Don't you worry about anything, you two are super stars."

I called Alice and she is super excited about spending time with Chelsea.

Alice is riding high on the kiss we shared last night. I can feel her through the phone, with the excitement in her voice. I think Alice is about to be where I am in this relationship, on top of the world. Alice let me know that Joe and Sofia had a great time last night. She told me they liked me and thought I had the potential to make her happy for the rest of her life. It was the best news Alice could give me.

When my lips touched Alice on her lips last night, it was like nothing I have ever experienced in my entire life. The deepness of my feelings at that moment goes beyond an average person's understanding. It's true that I have not been intimate with any woman for some time now and that could be why the intensity of Alice's lips left me breathless, but it is deeper than just that. It's as if I belong. It's a mental thing.

Right now, I'm on a sexual fast. I've made no sexual advance toward Alice even though the act with her would be, or should I say will be, the most intense experience of my physical life. What I want with Alice goes beyond physical, I want a relationship that will surpass the test of time, I want the extraordinary that life has to offer.

I have learned the meaning of restraint with the help of my psychologist and a lot of therapy. I admit that I'm crazy, but I can fix crazy with a lot of help from my doctor. I no longer live for the moment; I want to live for the future, for marriage and a family. I want a shared purpose in life with Alice.

Alice gave me a vision of what the future holds for us. I have a picture of my future for the first time in my life; I have goals.

Alice freed me from the frustration of seeing nothing change in my life. She introduced me to a different lifestyle. Alice brought to life the meaning of 1 Corinthians 13; "Love is patient, kind, not jealous, does not brag, is not arrogant, does not act unbecomingly, does not seek after its own interest, is not provoked, does not take into account a wrong suffered, does not rejoice in unrighteousness but rejoices with the truth, bears all things, believes all things, hopes all things, endures all things, and never fails."

Alice claims not to believe in God, yet she is everything that God loves in a person. She is what God wants all of us to be like. God gave Alice more than mere beauty; He gave her self-respect.

Alice is beautiful even though she doesn't think so, but it's her character that makes me love her more and more every single day, not her physical beauty. Alice brings closeness at an emotional level that is like a spiritual awakening. All my physical feelings are focused on Alice, not myself. I have tenderness for her that I never knew existed in my body. It is like an emotional awakening. I'm hoping my affection for Alice is contagious and becomes incurable for the both of us.

The doorbell rang and Jeff was on his feet before I had the chance to say, "She is here."
It was as if Jeff felt Chelsea's presence before she touched the doorbell.

Jeff said, "Hi Chelsea, give me a hug. You look great! Life must be treating you good."

Chelsea said, "College is great. I've learned to be independent and at the same time keep all those who I love in my mind. I feel good about my life right now and when you feel good, you look good."

Jeff said, "There is someone in the other room who is dying to see you. Come this way."

Chelsea said, "Ed, I am so happy to see you. Give me a hug."

I grabbed Chelsea and swung her around in a circle. Chelsea has the warmest heart of any individual I know. Pure sweetness describes her nature.

I said, "It's so good to see you Chelsea, it's been nearly a year since we have seen you. That's way too long, you need to come around more often, I have missed you immensely.

Chelsea said, "I've missed you also. School takes so much of my time; I don't even realize what I'm missing. When I graduate, I'm going to make up for all the lost time before I get a job. You may have to put up with me for a whole month."

I said, "We can handle that. Bring it on. We could never get too much of you Chelsea."

Chelsea said, "Jeff has been keeping me in the loop. I love spending time with you guys. I knew a handsome hunk like you wouldn't last too long in the single world. I just hope you made a good choice; the person you choose to spend your life with effects your mind. It can either make your life a dream come true or the worst nightmare you have ever had.

You know Ed that Hell can be right here on earth if you make bad choices. Weather you believe Hell is a place of pain and suffering, or a state of permanent separation from Gods presence, it is everlasting punishment. I believe Hell is a combination of physical agony and emotional torment that is the result of absence from God and His blessings.

You have been to Hell on earth in the past; I do not want you to go there again, ever. You made me a promise to protect yourself from beautiful women, and when you make a promise to a child and break that promise, the child takes it personal. Tell me you are not going to break my heart."

I said, "First of all, my lady's name is Alice and she is anything but beautiful. I'm past that stage of my life, I still admire beauty, I just don't lust for it. I've learned not to perform the act of love until I am in love. I want the good life; I now know it was a critical mistake to welcome the temporary gratification that beautiful women provided. I have found spiritual and physical love with Alice and it has revived my dying soul. I am passionately and hopelessly in love with Alice; just her touch makes me giddy with desire. It's impossible to over emphasize how dramatically Alice affects me. I can hardly wait for you to meet her. Jeff is going to cook for us tonight."

Jeff said, "That's right, you are at my mercy. I've been inspired by my brother's enthusiasm for life once again and I'm preparing a feast to celebrate the joy in his heart.

The main course is baked chicken breast in wild rice. The side dish is broccoli casserole and baked sweet potatoes.

The salad will have my special dressing made with olive oil, vinegar and Dijon mustard. The bread is a French loaf with butter and garlic. A meal fit for royalty."

I said, "That sounds perfect for Queen Alice and Princess Chelsea. You see Chelsea; I have fallen into the sublime realization of the amazing emotion called love. Until I met Alice, I always confused love with lust. I'm unable to control lust, however, with love, I found the need for self-restraint in order to control and tame the forces of nature in order to achieve a higher relationship. I have mastered the near-mystical union with all its emotional complexities. With love, there is no worry. You see worry causes me anxiety disorders and depression, which lead to substance abuse. I have conquered my demons.

My love for Alice has completely opened my emotional closet. I have achieved unconditional love. Alice makes me vulnerable to my feelings, I just let them out all over the place, and I have finally achieved emotional freedom. I always had problems expressing my emotions, but not with Alice, that's how I knew she was the one for me."

Chelsea said, "Looks like we are in for a very interesting evening. I'm excited to meet Alice. She is the one for you. My prayers have been answered. Your life is on the track to success with your future family. I'm excited for you Ed."

I said, "Thank you Chelsea Songbird, that means a lot to me.

You get to stay in my room tonight; I'm going to share Jeff's room. You have clean sheets, and the towels and wash cloths are in the bathroom for you."

Chelsea went to freshen up and I began to set the table. Tonight we will use only the best tableware with cloth napkins. As I set the crystal glasses on the table, I can't resist thumping one to hear the unique sound that only crystal makes.

I make a quick trip to the flower store for a dozen red roses. They will look beautiful with the white tablecloth and clear crystal vase. This may even jog Jeff's memory of when he first met Chelsea.

Jeff said, "The chicken will be done soon. I see a car pulling into the driveway, Ed, you may want to greet your guest."

I was out the door in a flash. My heart began to race as Alice opened the car door and stepped out. I grabbed her hand and guided her into my home.

I said, "Alice, this is my little brother Jeff and his friend Chelsea Songbird."

Everyone shook hands and exchanged small talk about how they had heard so much about each other.

I stood and watched everyone converse while taking in the beauty of Alice. She is so poised and polite. Her hair is in soft curls falling over her shoulder and her dress floats gently across her knees as she steps toward me.

Alice said, "Ed, where can I put my purse? I have some after dinner mints, can you put them somewhere?"

I said, "Let me put your purse in the closet and I will get a bowl for the mints. Oh, my favorite, chocolate mints."

Chelsea was talking to Alice about the roses on the table when Alice glanced out of the corner of her eye in my direction. It was as if she had a twinkle in her eye as a smile filled her face.

I don't know if my feelings are so strong because of my secondary virginity for the past years or if it is just because Alice is the one meant for me. With Alice I have it all. I stopped having sex and my life got better.

I see Alice blossoming like a rose bud with affection for me, every day I feel her deep sense of belonging to me only.

Jeff said, "Ed can you help me with this can opener, I meant to get a new one but it slipped my mind. I just can't seem to get it to turn."

Alice said, "Let me see it Jeff, I had trouble all the time with mine until a friend showed me a trick. Let's put just a couple of drops of vegetable oil on this can opener where the two wheels are. Now try it Jeff."

Jeff said, "That is amazing. It is like a brand new can opener. Thank you Alice."

Jeff poured the green olives into a bowl and placed them on the table. He looked at Alice and nodded his head with great approval of her help.

Jeff said, "Let's all sit down now; I want to say a little prayer for the food and friendship we are sharing this beautiful day.

Dear God, thank you for everything. My greatest desire is to belong; mankind was designed to have relationships with each other and you have given me the best people possible to share this dinner and my feelings with. I will do everything in my power to continue building relationships with these beautiful people you have put into my life. Amen."

Chelsea said, "That was moving Jeff. Now please pass me the bread. Everything looks delicious."

The meal truly was delicious and the chocolate after dinner mints were perfect. My mouth feels so fresh right now and I would love to share it with Alice.

It's time for Jeff and I to clear the table and clean the dishes. I escort the ladies to the living room while telling them how lucky they are to get out of cooking and cleaning. Both just giggled and as I walked back to the kitchen, I hear them talking about what good cooks Jeff and I are.

Alice said, "Chelsea you are so lucky to have a boyfriend who cooks for you and on top of that is a great cook, and cleans the dishes."

Chelsea said, "Jeff is not exactly my boyfriend even though he is a boy and a friend, we are just friends. Jeff is the first guy that gave me a crush. I call it a crush because I was only fifteen years old and too young to know what love means. That's what everyone says anyway. I could live my life feeling the way Jeff moved me and be completely satisfied."

Alice said, "Ed told me a little about your relationship with Jeff, both before and after the accident. I do hope Jeff makes a full recovery and his memory of your closeness returns."

Chelsea said, "I remember the day when Jeff woke up like it was yesterday. I felt so hollow when Jeff looked me in the eyes and had no idea who I was. He now accepts the fact that at one time we were close, but when he touches my hand those feelings that come with a crush are gone. It's a feeling of friendship, not love. I will always think what we had was my first love. I would be happy to feel that way until my last breath. It was amazing."

Alice said, "I hope his memory returns and you two live happily ever after. You make a great couple."

Chelsea said, "Thank you Alice, that's so sweet. I have put my feelings on a shelf right now; it's just gross to me to pine over someone who doesn't feel for me. I thank God every day for giving me the strength to control my feelings.

I protect my emotions with the love of my family and friends so I'm never starving for love. When one is hungry for food, they will eat almost anything, and when they are hungry for love, they will be with almost anyone. What people will do for love."

Alice said, "You are so spot on, just nineteen but beyond your years in wisdom. Ed told me you are a bright spot in his hazy life. Now I see what he was talking about. There's not a selfish bone in your body.

You know that Ed is pursuing me and that I'm keeping my guard up on my feelings for him. My feelings for Ed are like bees around a flower, they are all over the place. As you can see I'm not much to look at and Ed is God's gift to women. If I lost him, and let his love in my heart, it would ruin me for life. I just don't know if I can keep him interested for a lifetime.

I have a choice between the pain of rejection and the pain of regret. Am I woman enough to handle the pain if Ed dropped me for another woman? That is the million-dollar question. Do I take the golden opportunity of what we feel, right now this minute, and hope it will last a lifetime, or do I protect my heart from the pain of a future break-up?

It sounds a bit daunting to look into the future at the pain that could be just waiting to jump all over me. I'm so stoked up over Ed that I just don't see clearly what is right in front of me. It feels so right, it's like over the moon for me.

Ed's smile is what melted my heart the moment he first spoke to me. I've always thought that love at first sight was superficial love and would never last. That is stuck in my head and I just know I could never keep Ed happy, and he will eventually dump me.

I've experienced the loss of love with someone who I didn't feel half of the love that I feel for Ed. Darkness filed my life for months. It was the most painful experience of my life, completely unforgettable. I want more than love; I want love wrapped inside a relationship. I'm unaffected by superficial things, such as good looks, I'm worth more than my ugly looks; I'm confident and secure in who I am. Ed just happens to be blessed with a perfect body and a gorgeous face. We are such a mismatch in the looks department.

The men I have observed in the workplace or the ones my friends are with seem to think that as long as they are doing things for you, you should feel loved. They are completely oblivious to their woman's needs for daily affection. If they could notice a woman for any little change in her beauty, give her a hug, a peck on the cheek, grab her hand and give it a squeeze, just some sign of affection and a woman is in heaven daily.

You know Chelsea it is easy to be on the outside of love and look into your friends relationships, but when you are inside of love, you become blind to everything you have learned if you let yourself. I plan to keep my eyes wide open."

Chelsea said, "You know my sister Cloie is married to Jeff and Ed's brother, his name is Matt Hall. They are the perfect couple. They are being eaten alive by the love bug. When they first met over a live feed internet connection, there was an instant rush of attraction, just like what happened to you and Ed, and me and Jeff, when we first met. Visual chemistry is powerful enough to rock two people's world who are in different states, Oklahoma for Cloie and Texas for Matt. That's what the internet is capable of, spontaneous flirting that leads to the ideal partner.

I see the same thing between you and Ed that I saw in Cloie and Matt. It's as if you are under some kind of a spell, like you are walking on air. My sister Cloie was the same way when she saw Matt. There is no need to fight it Alice, just roll with it.

Just because Ed is so handsome, and you think you are not pretty enough to hold him, doesn't mean a wonderful relationship won't last the test of time.

First of all, beauty is in the eye of the beholder. Secondly, you are comfortable with your defects, they are part of who you are and Ed cherished each and every one of them. You are like no other girl that Ed has ever dated and he loves that about you. Alice, you have a magnetic charisma that makes you beautiful in your own unique way, you have the right sexual chemistry for Ed. Your superficial imperfections just don't matter to Ed. He told me so. I hope you let your heart lead you to your future and not your mind. I believe your heart will take you to the right place."

I said, "The dishes are done and I hope you two had a chance to get to know one another. You are my two favorite girls on earth. Can I get you something to drink?"

Chelsea said, "I'm good on the drink, I still have a half glass of tea. Ed, I want you to know that Alice is everything you said she was, pure class. I like her and I know we will be great friends."

Alice said, "Chelsea is way beyond her years as far as intelligence goes, and she feels deeply, I like that about her. Yes Ed, I could use another glass of tea."

Alice handed me her glass and I touched her finger as she released the glass into my hand. It was like an electrical charge that filled my body with pleasure. Alice felt it also for her eyes widened and began to twinkle.

Jeff said, "I'm so glad everyone enjoyed dinner, the way I know you liked it is because there are no leftovers. We all stuffed ourselves. If anyone needs desert, I have some ice cream in the freezer. Jest let me know. I thought we might play a game of Dominos."

Dominos is Jeff's favorite game. It helps him with his adding. Sometimes he takes a full two minutes to add the numbers together. He even uses his fingers to count on when counting dots on the Dominos.

While watching Jeff struggle to add the dots on the Dominos, my mind wanders, back to my days of playing football with the very helmet Jeff was wearing when his head hit the field and the helmet cracked. All the times that I was tackled and hit the dirt, why didn't the helmet crack with me wearing it? Why did it wait years later and claim my brothers mind?

If this accident would have happened to me when I was Jeff's age, I could have skipped the whole drug scene. All those wasted years in a stupor. Jeff would never touch drugs and if this tragedy had not happened to him, he would be in college right now molding his future. I guess there is a reason for things happening in the order in which they do, but I will never understand why.

Chelsea said, "I've had a wonderful evening, thank you so much for dinner Jeff and Ed. Alice, I'm glad we had the time to get to know each other. You are everything Ed said you were.

I really must get back to campus before it gets any later. I don't want to be the only person on the road."

I said, "You know Chelsea, I straightened up my room so you could stay in it tonight. Jeff is sharing his room with me."

Chelsea said, "I so appreciate your offer, and you are family since Cloie married your brother Matt but I just don't think it looks good for me to spend the night with two guys."

Alice said, "Chelsea, I totally understand but it is too late at night to be driving by yourself. I have an extra room and you are welcome to use it."

Chelsea said, "You're on. I really don't like driving this late at night, and I'm sleepy, with all that good food, it affects me."

The girls left and Jeff challenged me to another game of Dominos. As we played, Jeff would take a break and rest his mind. He would talk about what a good dinner he prepared and that slow cooking makes food taste better and he was glad because of his slow thinking. He can excel at cooking and it gave him a lot of pride.

I guess God has His own plan for each and every one of us and who am I to question why things happened to my brother.

Jeff said, "That Alice is something else. Do you have any idea how many can openers I have bought because they were too hard to operate? She is a genius, and I like her personality. She is down to earth."

I said, "Alice is unique and this is what attracts me to her. She doesn't need validation; she creates her own self-esteem internally. She doesn't mind sharing knowledge, teaching.

I'm addicted to her sexual energy all wrapped into her playfulness and she is totally unaffected by it all. It's natural for her.

My life is so changed by saying no to sin. Sin is a disease of the heart, of the mind and of the spirit. Sin is full of hate for yourself and all those around you. I've stopped running from God and I have told everyone I have hurt how sorry I am. I also told God I am sorry and he has forgiven me and gave me the most precious gift of all, Alice.

Addiction to drugs is my biggest sin; my addiction to love is my greatest gift. God gave me this gift, I thank him daily. I'm past my self-absorption in the world of drugs and beautiful women for my pleasures. I want a relationship to enrich my life for the long term. I'm in it for true love, a love that transforms both the giver and the receiver. I have to get Alice to the point of scary love like I'm in, so she will receive me.

I begged God to save me from drugs, and He did. Now I'm asking God for Alice's heart and I'm looking forward to His answer. I will live with whatever he wants for me. Little brother, you and Chelsea brought me back to God and I thank you for that. I'm glad you like Alice. Jeff, she will soon be your sister-in-law."

Jeff said, "That sounds great, you two are the perfect couple. Chelsea seems to like her also. Chelsea is a good judge of character.

By the way Ed, you know God is freedom, the devil is bounding. Give Alice all the freedom she can stand. A relationship should yield goodness and goodness brings happiness through the act of granting freedom. Courtship is the beginning of something beautiful. You and Alice should enjoy each other in your journey to the ultimate love."

Chapter 7
Alice and Chelsea

We all have a reason for existence. I couldn't see that in my self-absorbed drug induced stupor. My eyes are clear now and I see two beautiful women in my life, Alice and Chelsea. Before my eyes were open, I wouldn't have time for either one of them. I would be spending my time with beautiful women who could bring me instant pleasure. Everything was about my physical pleasure, which left me empty, hollow and in pain. My mind was my prison and I couldn't find the key. Nobody goes through life unscathed, but my self-destruction could have put me in an early grave. I'm not the only one affected by self-absorption, this is the "I" generation and many people will live empty lives. There is a loud silence of a drug induced youth in this country. The catastrophic effects will speak loudly in the future of this United States of America.

I've lived in both worlds and it is very difficult to get your innocence back once you've lost it. It is not impossible but difficult. When I become a doctor for pain management I hope to reach our youth before they cross the line; prevention is so much easier than trying to reclaim ones innocence. Not everyone in life will be blessed with two amazing women, like Alice and Chelsea, for a fresh start. I believe physical pain must be treated along with mental pain.

Chelsea said, "It is so kind of you to share your home with me Alice. I really didn't want to drive all the way back to campus. It's lonely when it is dark. I feel bad that Ed fixed up his room for me and I just didn't want to sleep in it. I did however take a shower and fix my hair so I got some use of his effort to comfort me."

Alice said, "You know Jeff and Ed are great hosts. I felt right at home. Jeff is smart and such a sweet guy. I'm sure he understands why you didn't want to spend the night with two guys, he wasn't the least bit surprised when you told them that you were going to drive back to campus tonight. However, he had a look of concern on his face that quickly vanished when you agreed to stay the night at my house. No one wants to see a young girl drive late at night for an hour and a half. You are right about Jeff being smart about life, the accident couldn't take that part of him away. It's what I like about him.

That's the part of Ed that I like the most; his intelligence. Most women would want him for his looks, which I appreciate, don't get me wrong, but I'll have to contend with beautiful women always trying to get his attention. It's very annoying. Ed is so good looking that I just don't think I will ever be exclusive with him. He will first have to earn my confidence, and then win my pride over, in order for me to feel at ease with his looks.

I'm a woman of high value even though I don't look like it. I will make a loyal teammate for some lucky guy. I'm not going to schedule my life around Ed just yet. I have to be sure he is ready for a long-term commitment before he receives my life. I'm not much for sharing my man with other women. By upholding to my standards, my self-worth is intact and my self-confidence is stronger than ever. I can't let a pretty face take all that away from me."

Chelsea said, "Ed is very good looking, I totally agree with you on that issue. I personally think his good looks are his downfall in life and he wants to change what it has done to him. Good looks can be a curse because everyone caters to you and you expect life always to go your way. In the real world, life continually throws you a curve ball that takes you for a spin. Ed learned this the hard way. Ed once told me, 'You must value yourself, don't let someone make your body their playground.' This is what happened to Ed and he was trying to spare me the pain of what he has experienced. Sin cannot bring peace of mind."

Alice said, "Thank you for sharing that with me. I now know that Ed is deeper than I realized. In my world, the things you consider sin I just think of as self-destructive. I'm just not into self-destructive behavior or as you call it sin, never have been. I'm lucky I never did all those rebellious things most kids do. I always strived for integrity; it is what appealed to me. Integrity is doing the right thing even when no one is looking; this gives me a feeling of self-respect. No one can take that away from me. It gives me a healthy high."

Chelsea said, "I'm starting to see why Ed is consumed by you Alice, you got it going on. Ed told me you are full of unbridled human passion. Your human passion is a direct result of your self-respect. You can see the big picture."

Alice said, "It sounds like Ed talks about me a lot."

Chelsea said, "Oh yes Alice, you are the main topic. I don't know if you and Ed will hook up for a lifetime or not, but I'm happy for Ed for as long as you two last. Ed is high on life instead of drugs for the first time since I've known him."

Alice said, "Sounds like I have a lot of responsibility for Ed's happiness. I accept this responsibility by dating him, however if I feel my life is at risk for my happiness and we are not right for each other, I will bail. I won't be a martyr for anyone. In my book, it takes two to tango. I have to feel good about myself in a relationship to stay in it. I don't like my emotions to take me to a dark place. Ed has a tendency to be nice to women who hit on him when he is with me. When it happens, I have no control over the heavy darkness that fills my body. I hate that feeling and it's very difficult to make it go away. It can last for hours or days. It's not jealousy, it's like I'm being slapped in the face when Ed enjoys the attention from women right in front of me. It's an insult to me. Ed's eyes are closed to my feelings on this subject. If he cannot open his eyes, we will never make it for a lifetime. I do not want a lifetime of darkness creeping into my life until it consumes me. Ed says he understands but no one really feels what I feel but me."

Chelsea said, "Alice you must make Ed understand what you are going through when he responds to women who just want to hump his body for fun. Ed really doesn't understand women. This is why he has so many problems with women. He hasn't a clue as to why they do what they do. There are a lot of game playing evil women in this world that are mind wreckers."

Alice said, "You are so right Chelsea. I can see it in their eyes especially when they strike up a conversation with Ed. When Ed responds they glance at me with such satisfaction that it makes my skin crawl. Evil is just shooting out of their eyes."

Chelsea said, "If you want Alice, I can explain all this to Ed. Maybe I will be able to make him understand. Ed has a lot of respect for my opinion. I took him through one crisis in his life, maybe I can reach him again."

Alice said, "Chelsea that is so sweet of you to offer to help. I would like to reach Ed on my own, but if I can't, I would love to call on you in the future. You have a talent for reaching Ed. However, if we are going to be a couple, we need to learn to solve our own problems, on our own. I need to find a way to reach Ed without looking like a jealous nut case.

Chelsea let's talk some about you and Jeff. What is

it about him that holds your attention?"

Chelsea said, "His personality for starts. He is very handsome and that doesn't hurt anything, I must admit when he first flirted with me, my jaw dropped. Good looks run in the family. His intelligence is what ultimately holds my attention even to this day. His loss of memory has not affected his ability to reason and learn.

When the time is right I will move on with my life. If there is a chance that Jeff will fall in love with me now, with no previous memory of me, I don't want to miss out. It's been over five years now so if someone new turns my head I will be able to move on. Until then, I'm watching for that spark to reignite between Jeff and myself. Right now, there is nothing more than friendship between us on his part. I'm hoping our friendship will last a lifetime and my feelings will turn to friendship only. I will be able to move on in my life eventually, I've promised myself that."

Alice said, "I wish you all the happiness life can bring Chelsea, you have a lot to offer and whoever gets you is a lucky guy. No need to be in a hurry, life lasts a long time. Get your college education so you never have to depend on anyone for support. I got mine in accounting and there is always a need for high paying jobs in that field. It gives me freedom to live the lifestyle I like.

Let education be your priority and the rest will follow; happiness, security and a mate for life."

The next morning we met at a restaurant for breakfast and all went our separate ways when we were done eating. Alice said I could call her in a couple of days and Chelsea told Jeff he could call her anytime; she would make herself available. We all had such a good time.

Chapter 8
Ed's Conversation with Jeff

When I unlocked the door, Jeff was standing in the hall to greet me. He took the bag of groceries from my arms and headed for the kitchen.

Jeff said, "Good choice, salmon, excellent source of omega-3 fatty acids. A healthy body makes for a healthy mind."

I said, "I need all the help I can get, no telling how many brain cells I killed with my drug adventure. I've used my youth up with hard drugs and now I'm old before my time. The magical power of love is upon me Jeff, and Alice tells me to call her in a couple of days. Why does she not understand that I want to be with her every day?

I entered the gateway that led to Hell in my drug stupor, a very dark place in my mind; it made my body so heavy at times I could not move. They call it depression. I never want to go there again. I need to get a handle on myself or get Alice in my life daily. I'm feeling things I never knew existed. I'm under the influence of Alice and I got it bad. Drug use makes you lose the ability to see around the corner; Alice makes me see my future, the rest of my life with her by my side. I have to find a way to show her we are meant to be one. She is my good dope. She is what I need for a lifetime.

You know Jeff, every experience in love adds to our character; I wish the first girl I ever loved was Alice. The drug scene would never have happened, the mindset I developed about women would never have happened, the wasted years would be filled with children instead of empty pain. My character would be unblemished, pure as a winter snow.

I have repented for all the wrong I have done, and God has blessed me with Alice, I just wish I had listened to God in the first place and skipped all the sinning the evil one placed in my heart. I know there are always repercussions in a relationship, and I ruined many women. I'm sorry for that. I was not a very nice guy. I was awful on so many levels."

Jeff said, "Don't beat yourself up. You have asked God for forgiveness and he has washed all your sins away. You are fresh. If you stay on track, God will guide you through out the rest of your life.

You know Ed, my instincts are good, I see you and Alice living the good life. Don't be in such a hurry you have your whole life to be with Alice. She knows your past. Changed behavior over a substantial period of time is how you build trust. Give her some time to be sure you will not backslide."

A heavy silence filled the room. My little brother just put me in my place. He is right; I'm always in a hurry for things I want.

In my past, a beautiful woman was like being addicted to a powerful drug, it was all I could think about. It is like a chemical in my brain, which I have no control over. It is my dark demon, being anxious. I want what I want now. I could chase Alice away with this behavior. Jeff is right; I need to give Alice some space.

I said, "Little brother I'm glad we had this conversation. I'm going to give Alice all the room she needs. You are so right, I'm about to blow it with the true love of my life. I'm trying to smother her just like every other girl, and they all left me because of it.

Alice asked me to contact her in a couple of days; I think I'll give her four days to think about me. I hope that she will be out of her mind wanting to talk to me, and she will call me in two days because she just can't stand it any longer. I'm no game player; I just need to be sure Alice has all the time she needs to be sure she wants to spend the rest of her life with me."

Jeff said, "That's a good idea, that is, if indeed you can stay away from Alice for four whole days without going out of your mind. We may have to get a straight jacket to confine you."

I said, "That's real cute Jeff. You know I'm a loose cannon, a straight jacket just might put me over the edge forever. You would feel responsible, and your conscious wouldn't let you put me in a nursing home. I can see you spoon feeding me and changing my diapers. Now wouldn't that be a lot of fun."

Jeff said, "On second thought, you are on your own, no interference from me. I have enough trouble just taking care of myself.

You know Ed that even after you marry Alice, you will need to give her time for herself. Some say that marriage is a tough road to go down. It's not always a rosy day. You assume the responsibility of the person you marry and yourself. That's double the responsibility you have now."

I said, "Little brother, I would take on anything that Alice wanted to put on me. There is no load to heavy that I wouldn't take on for Alice, and be glad of it. Jeff I can't even explain what is going on in my body and mind. I don't even know if any human being has ever felt what is going on with me. If I could put it in a bottle, it would sell for millions of dollars. I'm not exaggerating. This feeling is out of this world. It's all the time, even when I'm not with Alice I can feel her all around me. I can smell her and feel her soft skin on my hands. It's like she is here even when she is not. I just don't want any other man finding what I have and stealing it from me. Alice is a treasure chest full of precious jewels."

Jeff said, "You better be careful Ed, this woman has your nose wide open. She may be worse than that dope you snorted all those years."

I said, "Dope can't even touch what I feel for Alice. I'm telling you it's out of this world good. It's the first time I've ever felt true love. My mind is so clear it's like everything is in high definition. I think of Alice and words pop into my head like someone else is talking in my head. The words just appear. Let me show you little brother.
True Love
The truth about Love is found in the Word, the Bible is the Word.
Search the Word, find the truth
It's not all about me, now I'm selfless, I living in the truth
I too pay the price for true love
It's worth it
My lasting true love
Living in the truth
It's not all about me
It's all about you my true love
You're my everything
It's all about you, my truth
My lasting true love

You see what I mean. I could rap all day about Alice and have words left over. It's like endless thoughts about the meaning of true love. I never thought it even existed. It always seemed like a fairy tale to me. Something made up, a story to make you happy while you read it, not real.

True love is more real than the air I breathe into my lungs that keeps me alive. It's like magic, I'm in this bubble that can't be popped. I want to feel like this for the rest of my life.

You know Jeff, if I hadn't done so many drugs, I could live until I was at least one hundred and twenty years old. That's how old the oldest person on earth has lived. Imagine feeling like I do and living for one hundred and twenty years.

The Bible states in Genesis 6:3, "And the Lord said, My spirit shall not always strive with man, for that he also is flesh; yet his days shall be a hundred and twenty years." It is no coincidence that the Bible states facts of what is happening today. In my mind, God gave me Alice. I've been praying to God to give me the wisdom to make my life better. This is when Alice caught my eye. The reason I know Alice will be my wife is because of what the Bible says in Mark 11:24, "Therefore I say unto you, What things soever ye desire, whey ye pray, believe that ye receive them, and ye shall have them."

It's no accident that I found Alice, God led me to her. God has forgiven my sins and chased the evil one out of my life. God has given me more than I even knew existed on earth; He has given me Alice."

Jeff said, "Ed you finally get it. All answers come from God. Knock and the door shall open. Use the wisdom God has given you and give Alice the room she needs. I would hate for you to scare her off. She is fully aware of our feelings for her, it's time for Alice to make a move, when she is ready."

I said, "You are right little brother, it's in Alice's ball court now. I'm going to pray for the strength not to call her."

Chapter 9
Alice's Move

With Adam and Eve, the apple on the tree was shinny, plump and beautiful, not all dried up, wrinkled, and displeasing to the eye. Kind of like I'm good looking and this is why all the women want to be with me. I'm telling you, it's a curse to be handsome. Many an Eve has come on to me.

I've never chased a woman, they all chased me. Alice is the first woman that I've made the first move with and she rings my bell. I'm trying desperately not to scare her off. When women come on to me a little strong, I've been known to head in the other direction. Don't want to do that to Alice.

It has been two days since I've called Alice and I am trying to stay quiet in my mind so I can stay calm. I just want to hear her voice. I've picked up the phone ten times starting to dial her number and Jeff's words kept coming into my mind; 'Use the wisdom God has given you and give Alice the room she needs.'

The chemicals in my mind go wild every time I think about Alice. I want to deeply connect with Alice over the phone and tell her she is the woman of my dreams.

How can Alice possibly not feel what I am feeling right this moment? The feelings are strong for her and I'm sending them mentally so she will call me. I cannot take a chance of scaring her off by making the first move. It was her words, to wait a couple of days.

I don't want to snap and lose my mind. Thinking about sports should help, or reading a good book.

I have a good western book I've wanted to read and this is the perfect time to start it. Reading always calms my emotions. I get out of my life and into the life of the characters in the book.

Occasionally I catch myself drifting back into Alice's mind; I can feel her thinking about me, but I focus on the book. I've been reading now for five hours and can only remember bits and pieces of what I've read. It's like impossible to focus without Alice popping into my mind.

My phone is ringing and it's like a thunderbolt of lightning struck my heart. I gather my composure after four rings and answer the phone.

Jeff said, "Has she called?"

I said, "No, I thought you were her calling. I just hope you are right about all this little brother, I'm about to lose my mind in anticipation of Alice's call. If I'm dead in the morning, please tell Alice she is my everything. No woman can ever walk in her shoes."

Jeff said, "Something tells me you are going to survive. If Alice doesn't call in a couple of days I will personally go to her house and find out what is going on in her head."

I said, "I don't know if I can last a couple of days or not. I'm trying to read a western book and can't remember half of what I read."

Jeff said, "Continue reading and take deep breaths. I love to discuss books, so clear your mind so you can tell me all about those cowboys."

Two more days passed for a total of four days. My

mental withdraw has taken a toll on me. It is as if I am numb. I topped out. I went as high with my anxiety as possible and then just fizzled out. I am going through the motions at work but I am dead inside.

Alice just doesn't feel as strongly about me as I do about her. If she did, there is no possible way she could stand four days without some sort of contact.

Alice asked for a couple of days, which means two days, not four. Tonight I'm going to ask Jeff to intervene and call Alice. I need to know if I'm being dumped. I'm not strong enough to hear Alice say the words 'not interested.' My brother can say what is on Alice's mind and I will accept whatever message he has for me, just be gentle with the words is all I will ask of Jeff.

The workday has finally ended. Three people asked me if I was sick. I must have looked awful. I'm sick all right, love sick, the worst kind of sickness known to mankind.

Jeff has been on the phone since I walked in the door. I waved at him and pointed towards the kitchen; it is my turn to cook. I place two chicken breasts in a glass casserole dish and top them with seasoned breadcrumbs. I wrap two sweet potatoes in foil and place everything in the oven. Next, I make a salad with lettuce, kale and tomatoes. I splash some olive oil on top; pour two glasses of water and check to see if Jeff is off the phone.

Jeff motions for me to come closer and hands me the phone.

Alice said, "Your brother is a riot. He has me laughing so hard I'm crying. The way Jeff tells the story of Ron and Ryan, the identical twins, has me in stitches. The funniest story is where Ron got sick and asked Ryan to take his place on a date. Ryan promised not to kiss Ron's girlfriend, and she thought Ron was trying to dump her because Ryan kept pushing her away. The girl broke up with Ron because she wanted to do the dumping, instead of being dumped. Ron couldn't get her back no matter what he did. Ron never told her about Ryan because it was a deceitful thing he did. He was ashamed of himself."

I said, "These two were a pair to draw to no doubt about it. They looked so much alike I couldn't tell them apart and at that time I was around them all the time. Ron made a big mistake with her; she was a keeper. She was a good girl, like you."

Alice said, "Please don't go putting me on a pedestal, I may not be able to live up to what you have in your mind about me. After all, I don't know if I will ever believe in God like you do. That would have to make you think I'm not such a good girl."

I said, "The very core of my faith rests on the fact that man exists in the world to find and come to know God. You are not an atheist who thinks religion is a superstition that must be ridiculed and eradicated, you are just waiting for your eyes to open and God to introduce himself to you.

In Psalm 14-1:2, 'The fool hath said in his heart, there is no God. They are corrupt, they have done abominable works, there is none that doeth good. The Lord looked down from heaven upon the children of men, to see if there were any that did understand and seek God.'

Alice, I have great hope that someday you will seek God and He will show Himself to you. It's all up to you."

Alice said, "I love the way you always know where in the Bible to find quotes that fit a situation that is at hand. You have a great memory.

If or when I find God, you will be the first person I will tell. None of my friends ever talk about God like you do, even the ones that believe in Him. Maybe they are afraid I will be insulted, or just not understand what they are talking about, but you Ed have no fear. That's what I like about you, it's all out in the open. Even the way you feel about me. You are an open book."

I said, "I'm glad you know how I feel about you. Most women are crazy, Alice you are sane, and that is what I love about you. I'm not perfect, a long way from it, but I love everything about me. I owe that to God. He taught me to love myself so I can love others. Before I knew God as I do now, I suffered from chronic resentment and blamed everyone for it. Now I know the meaning of life is to love unconditionally. Before I gave God control of my life, I spent all my time in self-exploration of my vulnerability, being afraid of rejection. I can now accept rejection without trying to change the person that is rejecting me. If you ever decide you have had enough of me Alice, just tell me and I will disappear."

Alice said, "That's nice to know but my fear is that you will dump me when you wake up from whatever this is you are going through. I'm holding back with my feelings because some day a beautiful woman is going to take you from me and my life will be ruined. I may never be able to recover. I've seen people who suffer the loss of the love of their life. It's the saddest thing ever. I can't take a chance on becoming one of them."

I said, "You don't ever have to give me your all. I could be the happiest I've ever been in my entire life to just have what you are giving me now. What you are giving me now is more feeling of pure love than I've ever experienced in my entire life. It is more than enough for me."

Alice said, "You come on so strong with your words that I just melt like butter and make a big mess of things. Right now, my emotions are all over the place. You make me feel like I can compete with all the women who will always be after you. I will have to live my entire life feeling my ugliness every time a beautiful woman flirts with you."

I said, "Matthew 6-22:23, 'His passion turned to poison and took away his will to live.' Alice, that is where I was, with you this is where I will always be, I want to live to be one-hundred and twenty years old with you by my side."

Alice said, "You come on so strong. How can I possibly resist your words? You know so many verses in the Bible by heart. Sometimes I wonder how you do it. You quote the Old Testament as well as the New Testament. I thought Christians were only concerned with the New Testament. Why do you read the Old Testament?"

I said, "I'm impressed that you even know where the passages that I quote come from. To answer your question Alice, the Old Testament is a prophesy to the New Testament, it reveals the will or message of God. Everything in the Old Testament such as the sacrifice of animals leads to the sacrifice of God's son, Jesus our Lord, the Lamb of God, the last sacrifice. Instead of offering animals, we celebrate the last supper and Jesus is our offering. It all ties together. After all it is one book called the Bible."

Alice said, "Since I've met you I have been reading the Bible so I can get a better understanding of you as a person. I must say, they have had some wild parties in the Old Testament. I'm starting to think that this could be the greatest book ever written. A person could live by the values in this book and have very little problems in their life. The question I have is just how many people can live up to the rules?"

I said, "God is a forgiving God and all you have to do is ask for his forgiveness and truly be sorry for your sin and He will forgive you. If you are truly sorry, chances are, you will not commit that sin again.

I'm starting to sound like my brother Jeff, he is the one always preaching these things to me. Anyway, I'm flattered that you are reading the Bible to understand what I'm about. Who knows, by the time you read it you could become a believer."

Alice said, "You never know. I will say this, the Bible is very interesting and I'm enjoying the read. From what I'm getting out of the Bible, it is not what you believe, it's what you obey. There are many different beliefs so I'm saying if you obey the laws in the Bible you will be safe.

If I become a Christian, the Bible will be my guide. I can't see how anyone can go wrong if they read the Bible theirself. The Bible would be the filter for my actions. You know the way I think about life is very much like what I'm reading in the Bible. My motto has always been to treat others as I want to be treated."

I said, "Alice, I want you to know that God created you just for me. Somehow, I just know this. You are my gift for returning to God. If I never see you again you will always be in my mind, and the gift of just knowing you, is enough."

Alice said, "I've never known anyone who can lay it on so thick. How am I supposed to resist you?"

I said, "You're not. Alice you are meant to be with me. You make me happy. God will make me have what I've never had, which is happiness, because I'm in His favor. God sent you to me."

Alice said, "Infatuation is blinding and I need to get to know you better with a clear mind. The reason I called was to see if you wanted to go to the zoo this weekend. The weather forecast is great, 75 degrees and no wind. What more can you ask for?"

I said, "What time can you pick me up?"

Alice said, "How about 9:00 a.m., we can grab some breakfast on the way. I would like a blueberry smoothie. I'll see you Saturday morning."

Chapter 10
The Zoo

I have not been to the zoo in years, and I am looking forward to spending time with Alice doing something that she suggested. It feels good letting Alice take the lead role in our relationship; it takes a lot of pressure off my shoulders. If Alice picks what we do then she is sure to have a good time. Women like having their way.

It wouldn't matter what we do as long as I'm spending time with Alice. That's what love does to you. You are just happy all of the time. Everything and anything makes you happy as long as the one you love is with you. It took me twenty-seven years to find this out and I'm going to do everything in my power to protect our love. The way I feel is magical, nothing in life has ever compared to this.

Sure, temporary feelings can make you feel good with drugs, but the word temporary is short lived. Being with a beautiful woman is temporary when it's just her beauty you are interested in. The good feeling passes with both, shortly.

I now know why I did drugs. I wanted things that just were not right for me. I wanted beautiful women and I wanted to control them. That combination just does not work. Because I couldn't get my way with them, I used bondage, which made things worse. When everything fell apart I became depressed, and my way out of sadness was drugs, but they pushed me even lower into depression when the high wore off. I became caught up in the vicious cycle of the demons of addiction. I remind myself of those days on a regular basis so the devil cannot steal anymore of my life.

I can finally see this precious gift of life God has given me. I can now see how the devil has tried to destroy this gift and I allowed him in my life to ravage my God given perfect body with drugs. I'm so ashamed of my behavior. It's like I live a double life and by living in evil for so long, I can now recognize it when it comes creeping around and I can smash it before it takes hold.

My life is now mature and in love with Alice. I will never live in the pain drugs can cause again. There were times when I was in such pain I could not understand how the rest of the world goes on. Now when I reflect on my past, I wonder how I could have ever let the evil drug pusher enter my life. Evil people can bring out the evil in you; this is why you must avoid them.

God in his magnificence has given me a second chance. He has shown me that life is a state of mind and I am choosing love to rule my mind.

Today Alice is taking charge of our relationship and I'm slowing it down a notch or two just to see where it goes.

The doorbell rang and when I opened the door there was Alice, wearing blue jeans, tennis shoes, and a white weatherproof jacket with a pink and white polka dot blouse. Her hair was pinned up on top of her head with a pink clip and she had on dark sunglasses. Alice looks very fashionable. I just stood in the doorway drinking up her presence.

Alice said, "Are you ready to go?"

I said, "Would you like to come in for a cup of coffee and a bagel? I like to toast the bagel with a pad of butter."

Alice said, "Sounds good to me. I'll need the energy to see the whole zoo; it's a three mile walk. Would it be ok if we stopped for a blueberry smoothie on the way, it can be my lunch?"

I said, "Sure. Let me take your jacket, Jeff turned the heat on before he left this morning. Let me warn you, he also made the coffee, and it is strong. He said to tell you hello."

Alice said, "Tell him I'm sorry I missed him and thank you for the strong coffee, that's the way I like it."

As Alice sat down and began to take off her sunglasses, I got weak at my knees. She looked up at me and I felt a warm sensation like I was melting. Not seeing her for a few days has heightened my senses, she is five feet from me but it feels like she has her arms and legs wrapped around my entire body. I am trying to slow it down but it is impossible in her presence. Alice is in command of my entire mind, body and soul. I have never felt such a presence in my entire twenty-seven years on earth. It's a different feeling from the darkness of lust, it's a light feeling of joy and happiness, and it feels pure and good. At this moment I do not dare touch her for I may explode with joy; that is hardly slowing it down a bit. I'm in a trance, just drinking in the beauty of my Alice sitting at the table in my house when she said, "I take my coffee black." I felt my eyes blink and suddenly I'm back, with my mind on coffee and bagels. My body is light and my feet are barely touching the floor but I do have control of my mind now as I pour us each a cup of coffee and toast the bagels.

I said, "How was your week Alice?"

Alice said, "Very confusing, I'm still trying to figure out why you haven't called me. I'm not sure if you are trying to tell me that you are moving on or if you are the kind of guy who doesn't say good-bye but just stops calling. Can you tell me what's going on with you?"

I said, "Alice, I will always want to talk to you and see you when you will let me. You make life so much more than I ever knew was possible. I didn't know I was capable of the feelings you have stirred up in me.

I'm being very careful with our relationship. I never want to regret anything, or want to redo anything concerning us. I want to make all the right moves, no regrets. I won't let lust ruin our future life together. Lust makes a person push their self on another. It makes a person wear out their welcome. You needed some room so I gave it to you. I hope you never hesitate to call or come see me for you will always be welcome in my world

The words of your mouth are like a strong wind that blows me off my feet. You are in total control of our life together. We will never let layers of problems mount up on us, let's solve them immediately, that is how we will protect the love we have. You felt we had a problem in our relationship and that is why you called me, and came to my house today. I want to be one-hundred years old and look at you the way I do this very moment."

Alice said, "There you go again, laying it on thick. How am I supposed to keep a clear and objective mind when you keep blowing it with such strong words? I want a clear understanding of what our future will be before you have a chance to break my heart."

I said, "If you never wanted to see me again Alice, that would be okay, because of you Alice, I finally know what life is meant to be, it's all about true love, which brings lasting happiness, not temporary pleasure, but a lifetime of continued happiness. I looked for the kind of happiness you bring me in the world of drugs. Now I realize that drugs are for people who cannot find love and just don't know how to have a good time. They are losing their soul to the world of drugs, which leads to the destruction of their mind and health. I wish everyone could find someone like you Alice; if they could, there would be no addicts in the world. Alice, you are the greatest girl ever."

Alice said, "There you go again. How can I ever live up to all that you think I am? You are putting an enormous amount of pressure on me to live up to your expectations. I'm just an ugly girl who tries to look the best I can with nice clothes, curled hair and makeup. I have never let myself get too close to anyone because I've seen the devastating effect of the break-up that some of my friends have experienced. It can ruin your life. I have made a very safe environment for myself with my married friends and family. I care deeply about both and they are safe.

What I'm trying to say Ed, is that if I let myself go with you and your feelings, I could enter into a place I've never been. I'm dipping into it now and then already but I pull myself back to reality before I get to the point of no return. It scares me. I've never known the depth of love that you could take me to. My mind has not ever gone there with anyone before. It is so heavy and deep that I become immobile. I cannot move. It's like I've had a mental breakdown. I could wind up in a mental institution, disabled or mentally ill for the rest of my life. You know people do have breakdowns. If I let myself feel for you what I'm capable of and you left me, I don't think I could function in the world anymore like I do now. That is the effect you have on me. Can you take on that kind of responsibility? I totally understand if you take off running right now; I'll just lock the door behind me when I leave."

I said, "I just have two words that say everything you need to know; you're safe."

Alice said, "In that case, let's go to the zoo."

I am so glad Alice could share her feelings with me. Now I know how to deal with her. I know she is fragile, easily damaged or broken. I can now take great care not to damage her mind or break her heart in any way over any little thing, not that I ever would. Now I can be more mindful and aware of her fears. I can offer her comfort and assurance if she feels intimidated by the outside world when we are together.

I am so accustomed to women who have all the confidence in the world that beauty gives them, that I didn't even think of Alice as being intimidated by the outside world of people. What Alice doesn't get is that she is the most beautiful person in the world to me. Somehow, I have to get that in to her head. She has to know I will never hurt her or leave her.

I don't know why Alice cannot see that I'm the fragile one in this relationship. After everything I've told her about myself you would think if anyone were to break, it would be me, not her. I am however, taking in her concerns and plan to lighten up on my intense feelings for her. I now know that Alice can feel my emotions. Sometimes I can barely handle them myself. I will dial things back just because Alice needs things to slow down. She can have them full speed ahead anytime she wants them.

Alice is in control of this date, she is even driving her car. The conversation is light; what went on at work, and how we spent our evenings away from each other. What would normally seem like a boring conversation feels like heaven just hearing Alice's voice. I am just so happy to be in the car with Alice, I'm hanging on to every word she utters. Me and my Alice, going to the zoo, what more can a guy ask for.

I can tell Alice is gaining confidence in herself. By telling her, 'You're safe', she now has trust in me, she knows I will never hurt her. She only has to deal with her own feelings of inadequacy. Things she creates in her mind.

Alice said, "We're here. That did not take long. I'll bet the animals are all in good moods today, the weather is perfect."

I stepped in front of Alice to purchase tickets to enter the zoo. She did not fight me on this one; I think she knew she would lose.

I grabbed Alice's hand and through the gates we went. It is a very large zoo but everyone had the same idea and the place is jumping with all kinds of people. You can feel the high energy of the crowd. Spring has a way of doing that to everything. The flowers are in full bloom and the animals are roaming around in their cages, not sitting in the corner waiting for the day to pass.

Alice said, "Can we go down that trail, it is less crowded, I want to be able to see the animals without having to look over other peoples shoulders?"

I said, "Sounds like a good plan, I love looking at the birds."

As we walked the winding trail, a snow-white peacock bird strolled out of the bushes right in front of us. He began to put on a show by spreading his tail and walking in circles. He is beautiful; his white feathers shine like they have a gloss on them. We froze in place as he stretched his neck to see if we had food in our hands. When he realized we did not, he strolled back into the bushes and soon was out of sight.

We look at each other with a smile on our faces like, 'wasn't that neat,' and continued down the trail.

Alice pointed at a pen full of red parrot looking birds; they were sitting on people's arms. We headed for the door to their pen and a young lady was selling nectar in small paper cups for the birds to drink. I bought one for each of us and we walked into their pen. Soon we both had birds all over our heads, shoulders and hands. They were taking turns getting a sip of the sweet nectar.

Alice pointed at my head and started laughing at me. I felt at least five birds on top of my head; their little feet were walking all over my hair.

Alice said, "If we stay in here much longer I believe those birds will take up residents on your head. You look like a British soldier with those birds on your head and shoulders. Hold that pose; I want to take a picture on my cell phone."

Alice is having a great time. I think it did her a lot of good to share her fears about our relationship. Her openness to talk about her feelings assures me that we will have a perfect life together.

I said, "You are very cute with your feathered hat yourself. Come over here and take one of those selffie pictures of us side by side. We can show our kids what fun we had."

Alice said, "There you go again, just in case you are right about us, Junior would get a kick out of these pictures. I have always wanted a son."

Alice is lightening up a little and having fun with my feelings for her. This is progress. She might as well get comfortable with the idea; someday she will be my wife. That is a fact.

The one thing I have learned from Alice is that you cannot force a relationship into being. If it doesn't come naturally it just will not work. Our feelings for each other are natural and mutual. All I have to do is gain Alice's trust. I must admit, if Alice had my background I would be very careful with my feelings. I understand why she wants to take it slow, what if I reverted to my old ways. I know that will never happen, but Alice doesn't know that. I've declared war against evil and I will never self-medicate my jealous heart. The drugs took my soul deeper than hell itself; my mind was broken and my heart fractured. I will never let evil do that to me again.

Alice has given me a new love of life wrapped in emotional vulnerability. She has changed my dark skies to iridescent blue. I will never lose what Alice has given me. She could live only in my mind for the rest of my life and that would be enough.

I said, "Enough of these birds, we have a lot of ground to cover, besides, one of them messed on my arm."

Out the door we went, and down the trail to the reptiles. Inside this building were snakes twenty feet long. Every color in the rainbow and they could look you right in the eye and stick their tongue out at you and never blink. Snakes are my least favorite critter on earth. They make my skin crawl. I was glad to get out of there.

Around the corner were two very large turtles. There is a sign with their names, Herman and Zelda.

Alice said, "How romantic, they are making love. They don't seem to be shy about it."

I said, "They don't exactly have much of a choice, there is nowhere to hide."

Alice said, "Herman is quite the lover boy, he had Zelda's eyes rolling into the back of her head. If I didn't know better I would say there is a smile on Zelda's face. Are you blushing Ed? This sort of thing is natural, and as you said, there is no place to hide.

Herman is a real Romeo, he is taking his time and Zelda loves it. This must be why the turtle won the race with the rabbit. The rabbit hits it a couple of times and it is over. I never gave it much thought, but I believe this is what they were trying to tell us in the story. The turtle wins the love race.

Tell me Ed, are you like the turtle in bed?"

I said, "I will be whatever you want me to be. Something tells me we won't have any trouble in that department."

Alice said, "When will I get to find out?"

I said, "On your wedding night."

Alice said, "That could be a long time from now."

I said, "I have all the time in the world as long as you are with me. I guess that makes me kind of like Herman the turtle, I am in no hurry."

Alice said, "Take a lesson from Herman today, that's just how I want it, only not in public."

We were watching Herman and Zelda for ten minutes and they were still going strong when we left. I couldn't believe I blushed, it is not the kind of thing you can hide, turning red. I've never seen two turtles go at it.

Alice did not seem to have any problem with it. I think she would have stayed until they finished if I did not start walking off.

Alice said, "Are you serious about not trying us out to see if we are compatible in bed before we get married? In this day and time it is just normal to make sure we are happy with each other in that department."

I said, "There is no doubt in my mind that we will be very happy in bed together. Besides, don't you want to look forward to that special moment on your wedding night?"

Alice said, "Yes."

Now, since that is settled, we can tour the rest of the zoo.

Alice grabbed my hands, looked me in the eye, got on her toes and kissed me. I gathered her into my arms, and now I'm the aggressor, I pull her mouth towards mine with my hand on the back of her head, I feel her body melt into mine as our lips lock.

As we pull apart, Alice regains her composure and a smile comes across her face. I grab her hand and we begin walking with sparks flying through our bodies. Just holding hands is electric.

I said, "Look Alice, there is the aquarium. It's my favorite, I love all the colors the aquatic animals and plants are blessed with. It's like going to the ocean and snorkeling, only you don't get wet.

Look, there is a starfish and a seahorse. The seahorse is the most amazing fish to me. The way they swim erect and having a horse like head, and a body covered with bony plates. I never get tired of watching them.

There is a sea otter; you know they are nearly extinct. Most live in the northern Pacific coast.

Oh look, there is a seal; you know some leather jackets are made from the hide of the seal. I like the way they swim so fast with their streamlined body and limbs modified into paddle like flippers. I bet they can swim thirty miles per hour."

Alice is in ah of all the beauty the fish possess and she is excited because I'm so excited to see them. It is like we feed off of each other's energy. That's the way it is suppose to be.

We spent at least an hour looking at all the fish but now it's time to move on to where the crowd is; we are going to see the elephants.

Alice said, "Look Ed, they have a baby elephant. Isn't it cute. I wish I could scratch him behind his ear. I bet he would like that. I wonder how long it took that male elephant to grow all that Ivory. It truly looks dangerous. There is the giraffe, now that is a strong looking African mammal with short horns. They like looking you in the eye; that tells me they are ok. Most people can't look you in the eye. Giraffes take a long neck to a whole new level. I bet there is a whole lot of neck kissing going on between those two."

Alice is making all kinds of comments leading to intimacy. I hope I remain strong enough to resist her advances. Spring has a way of stirring up natural feelings and Alice is hard to resist.

I said, "Now that we have seen most everything in the zoo, and the crowd is getting bigger, let's call it a day and grab a bite to eat. I know where a charmingly old-fashioned hamburger restaurant is that still toast their buns. It's a short drive from here."

Alice agreed, for we had spent several hours at the zoo.

Alice said, "This little restaurant has a certain charm to it. I'll just bet this is the original wood floor and bar. They are kept in top shape, a lot of tender loving care. The table and chairs are right out of the 50's. How about we sit at the bar?"

Alice can do anything she wants, and I think she knows that now. Her shy ways are rapidly disappearing. Alice has finally got the picture that her looks are not a factor in the way I feel about her. They were only a factor in her mind. Today she has conquered her fears. They may return tomorrow, but today Alice has control.

We ordered two cheeseburgers and tea. We both wolfed them down, that's what a lot of walking will do to you, give you an appetite.

I said, "Alice, how would you like to go to church with me tomorrow? It lasts for about an hour and then there is a luncheon afterwards. I would like for you to see the church we are getting married in."

Alice said, "You know I've been reading the Bible so I can understand you better, I think church is a good idea, it should be a real eye opener. I can't promise that I will join your church or be able to relate to your congregation but I'm willing to give it a try.

Ed, you are a really good person and I've got to be real with you. By now, we both know I have a problem with you being so good looking, and me being so ugly. The only way I'm able to deal with this is by treating it like a fairy tale. I decided to enjoy my time with you but at the same time realize that it could all end and go up like a puff of smoke and just disappear like smoke does in the air. I just can't give you my all until I'm ready. This is the only way I can deal with my emotions.

What if you wake up one day and are ashamed of the way I look, and what if a beautiful woman who is a good person comes on to you and you realize you could have the whole package? You know not all beautiful women are bad people."

I said, "Alice, you are the most beautiful person I've ever known, please never forget that."

Alice said, "Ed, it's because you make me feel beautiful. It's all because of the way you make me feel when I'm with you, or away from you, because you are in my mind. In other words, you are always with me and I feel so beautiful inside and outside. I just don't know how I can possibly go back to the ho-hum life I had before you became part of my life. I don't know if it could ever be enough now. I look back at my life before you and think how sad it is that I accepted that nothing existence, as my life."

I said, "That is what love is all about, a higher existence. I feel the same way you do Alice, only my life before you was pathetic and an inadequate existence. You had a life and you were happy with it. I have never been happy except as a child until I met you. You make me feel like a ten year old in a candy store. I want to feel this way for the rest of my life and only you Alice, can do that for me.

It is fine with me if you want to treat us as a fairy tale. This is one fairy tale that will come true for both of us if you let it. The ball is in your court and you have total control over the outcome. I'm 100% in so it's all up to you."

Alice said, "In all the existence of human kind, I don't know if anyone has ever laid it on this thick. Can you even see what I have to deal with here?"

I said, "I'll pick you up at 10:00 a.m."

I am willing to play the part in Alice's fairy tale, anything just to be near her.

Chapter 11
Church

I am fully aware that Alice believes that there can be no proof of the existence of God but does not deny the possibility that God exists. Alice lacks in faith. You must have faith to know God.

I personally believe the best place to meet God is in His home, the church. I'm honored to introduce Alice to God.

I had on my best shirt and tie, polished shoes, and every hair in place. It is time to pick up Alice. My heart is beating fast as I start the car. If Alice finds God today, it will make everything perfect in our relationship.

As Alice walks out the door and locks it, I'm right behind her. I grab her hands and tell her how lovely she looks as she turns to face me. She blushes and tells me that today she is dressing for God. If he shows Himself to her, she wants to look her best. For Alice this is showing her sense of humor. That's what I love about her.

It is a thirty-minute drive and Alice is telling me about the parts of the Old Testament that she is reading. She lets me know there is nothing new under the sun. People knew how to party thousands of years ago just like they do today. She has a point; people will always be people. Everyone is looking for a good time and some will do anything for a buzz.

When we arrived, people began shaking my hand and asking, "Who is this lady with you today?" I introduce Alice and she received a very warm welcome. I always sit close to the front of the church because it just feels right. I get inspired by just showing God that I want to be close to Him.

The message today is about lust and the harm it does to one's spirit.

Preacher Charlie said, "In the book of James 1:12-16; 12 'Blessed is the man that endureth temptation: for when he is tried, he shall receive the crown of life, which the Lord hath promised to them that love him. 13Let no man say when he is tempted, I am tempted of God: for God cannot be tempted with evil, neither tempteth he any man. 14But every man is tempted, when he is drawn away of his own lust, and enticed. 15Then when lust hath conceived, it bringeth forth sin: and sin, when it is finished, bringeth forth death. 16Do not err, my beloved brethren.' In addition, Romans 8:13 states 'For if ye live after the flesh, ye shall die: but if ye through the Spirit do mortify the deeds of the body, ye shall live.'

Today we have a 50% divorce rate because people are not living through the Spirit. Lust has become an acceptable lifestyle. You see it daily on TV, in movies and in advertisement. The clothing in stores, offered to our children at very young ages, barely covers their body. The message is to look lustful and be sexy.

Lust is an unending drive that needs more and more and is never satisfied. An example is the porn that drives an addiction that can never be filled. The person just wants more and more and is never satisfied.

With love, the spirit is satisfied and can be fulfilled with making love to one's spouse. Lust does not rule their life and consume their every thought.

The evil one is out to get our children and we must

arm them with the knowledge of his ways if we want them to grow up and have a healthy marriage. What we teach our children today will rule their life tomorrow."

Alice looked at me with a very pleased look on her face. As I grabbed her hand and gently squeezed it, I could feel the love flowing from Alice's hand into my entire body. Her love has a sweetness that calms my mind. Right now, I am so full of love that I must share my feelings with the world. It took me many years to learn the difference between lust and love.

It's not that my parents didn't try to tell me about the ways of the world, I just didn't listen. I fell into the way of the evil one with a lustful heart. It was all about women providing gratification with their beauty. I used their beauty to fulfill my lustful eyes but I was never fulfilled. I was caught up in the empty cycle of lust.

I totally understand the message that Preacher Charlie is delivering today because I have lived that life and I have found the life of truth with Alice, true love.

You see, lust breeds lust. You are never satisfied. You keep pouring yourself into a feeling that feeds your flesh that never is full. It is always empty and if one marries a person out of lust instead of love, then they begin to lust for a different person when the lust runs out for their spouse, then they wind up getting a divorce.

With love, it is different. Love is forever. When you truly love someone, you love them forever. Just like God loves us no matter what we do.

Preacher Charlie told the congregation to go in peace and he would see us in the meeting room to share coffee and donuts.

Alice said, "I enjoyed myself in this little church. Are we going to have a cup of coffee?"

I said, "Anything you want Alice."

We slowly strolled in the direction of the meeting

room when Preacher Charlie put his hand on my shoulder and said, "Who is this lovely lady with you today?"

I said, "Charlie, this is the love of my life, Alice."

Preacher Charlie said, "I have heard a lot about you Alice. You bring out the best in Ed."

Preacher Charlie put out his hand for Alice to shake and she took his hand into both of her hands and shook his hand.

Alice said, "It's so nice to meet you, it was a wonderful message you delivered today."

Preacher Charlie said, "It is God's message, I just read from God's book. God has given us a road map to happiness, all we have to do is read it and follow it. It is so simple I can't imagine why every soul on earth doesn't take advantage of this opportunity. It is the greatest gift we will ever receive."

Alice said, "I'm in the process of reading the Bible now; it is a very large book, it will take me some time to get through the whole thing. It is crammed full of messages. I have to read it slowly then digest what I read. In other words, for me it is a slow process."

Preacher Charlie said, "Sounds to me like you get the picture, one must take it slowly to absorb the entire message. Many times it's like a message inside of a message."

Alice said, "Yes you are right, and sometimes one chapter expands the message from the previous chapter. I find it fascinating."

Preacher Charlie said, "I'm so glad to have meet you Alice, and Ed, thanks for bringing her. I must get to mingling now. Enjoy your donuts and coffee."

Alice glanced up at me and a smile came across her face. Words are not necessary sometimes and Alice's smile told me all I needed to know. She is enjoying herself.

The congregation is very friendly and many had the chance to meet my Alice today. She must feel like a superstar. I've never brought a woman to church with me before and Alice has everyone's curiosity stirred up. She must feel like the Bell of the Ball right now.

I'm stepping back and letting her take it all in. She is handling herself very well for a stranger. You would think she has been going to church her whole life. She is a perfect fit.

I said, "Alice, I'm so glad you enjoyed yourself today. You are always welcome to join me in worship. I want you to have an open invitation even if I don't ask you to go. I'm not pushy when it comes to attending church."

Alice said, "I appreciate that. I can see where religion is a very personal part of a person's life and when I've made up my mind about it I will let you know."

We see things so much alike. We give each other all the room we need, and that feels so right. I just want to jump up and holler, I am so happy right now.

Alice said, "Did you ask Preacher Charlie to give a sermon on lust today?"

I said, "No Alice I didn't, however he did know I was bringing you today, and he knows how I feel about you. He also knows my past and Charlie has a way of preaching that touches on real life situations of his congregation.

Last month a young couple lost their five-year-old son in a car accident. Charlie preached about all the little people who go to heaven early in life so they can look after their parents on earth. He made a profound connection between heaven and earth and told each of us to talk to the angels in heaven for they are God's gift to watch over each of us. You see Alice, there is a mental connection between heaven and earth and the little ones up there are always listening to us, all we have to do is talk to them.

Preacher Charlie told the young couple to close their eyes and picture their son in heaven with his arm stretched out to pull them into heaven with him. He asked the couple to picture this every time their heart breaks from the loss of their son. Charlie reminded them that all of our stays on earth are short, but heaven is never ending. He asked them to picture their son sitting in God's house playing with his favorite toy. He told them how their son is safer now than he could ever be on earth. The evil one will never have a chance to tempt him. The message Charlie gave them that day gave them peace of mind.

That's just who Preacher Charlie is. He tries to touch the situations that his congregation is living in. In this little church, we all know what is going on in each other's life. It is important to us to share our burdens so others can help carry them for us. It just lightens the load.

What can I say; Charlie just knows how to reach us. After all, he has the Man helping him."

Chapter 12
Lucy Comes to Town

There is a knock on the door and when I open it there stands Lucy. She is even more beautiful than the last time I saw her. That could be because the last time I saw her she was locked in my bedroom for three days and had no makeup.

I said, "Hello Lucy, what are you doing knocking on my door?"

Lucy said, "I saw you driving down the street and followed you. I haven't seen you in years and just wanted to say Hi."

I said, "It's best we don't talk, things just were not good between us. I know it was my fault but we are not good for each other. It is best if you just leave."

Lucy said, "I've been married and divorced twice now so maybe it was partly my fault. I've grown up a lot since you've seen me. I have a two-year-old daughter to pick up in thirty minutes from daycare; I just want to talk to you until then."

I said, "I don't think that's a good idea, my life is very different now, I'm not the guy you knew."

Lucy said, "You are just as handsome as the day I met you, maybe I will like your new personality change and that way I could have the whole package. Won't you let me come in and meet the new you?"

Lucy removed her sunglasses and her beautiful blue eyes once again had my undivided attention. I could feel my body filling with the lust we once had. I shake my head and come back to my senses. The evil one had me for a moment. He just crept into my body and started a fire in my heart. How could I possibly let him creep into my mind and take control. I'm in love with Alice and right now I'm ashamed of what I just felt.

I said, "Lucy you need to leave right now. What we had is over, my life is going in another direction and you are only going to be in my past."

Lucy said, "I felt you when you looked into my eyes, the same feeling we shared when we were together. It felt every bit as strong. My legs are shaking right this moment. Can I just come in and sit for a moment?"

Lucy just walked past me and entered my home. She brushed up against me and I became weak as a kitten. I'm fighting these feelings with all my might but they are rolling over me like a tidal wave. What am I going to do? I can't have her in my home. I leave the door open, step out on to the porch, and sit on a chair. I'm not going into that room with Lucy. After a couple of minutes, Lucy comes on to the porch and sits in a chair next to me.

Lucy said, "You know how you always called me juicy Lucy? That's how I am right now. That's the effect you have on me, even after all these years. If you come inside I will let you feel what I'm talking about."

I said, "I'm not that person anymore. You are just as beautiful as you ever were, and yes, I do feel what you feel, but I'm in love with a girl named Alice, and I was only in lust with you Lucy. There is a huge difference between the two. I wish you love in your future but you really must leave now. Lucy, there is nothing here for you. We are part of each other's past and that is where we are going to stay. Our relationship was destructive. I became a drug addict and you have been divorced twice. We are just not meant to be together."

Lucy said, "You say you have changed, well so have I. No man has touched me for six months. During that time, I reflected on my past. The only person I truly loved is you Ed. I was happier being locked in your bedroom for three days then I've been with all the other men I've been with. I was young when we were together and I thought I was missing out on life. I wanted to flirt with guys and get all the attention I could. I'm grown up now and I know what I want. I want you Ed, and you won't have to lock me in your room, I want to be with you only. I knew it the minute I saw you driving. All those wonderful feelings came rushing through my entire body. Please give us a chance. Two dates and if you don't feel what I feel, I will move on."

I said, "Hold it Lucy, I told you I'm in love with Alice. You want me to throw her to the side while I date you. Girl, that's messed up. You have not changed; you are still putting yourself first. Do you have any idea what it would do to Alice if I went out with you? She would never get over it. It would ruin what we have. No Lucy, will you please leave now."

Lucy said, "Is she pretty, is she younger than me? Can she make you feel like I make you feel?"

Lucy started rubbing my arm and before I knew it, her lips were pressing against mine. My entire body went limp. Lucy's passion is as strong now as it was the day I met her. No wonder I locked her in my room, afraid someone would steal this magic woman from me. As our lips parted Lucy's sweet breath filled my senses. I pulled her close, our lips locked again, and my entire body was floating in lust. I didn't want the moment to ever end.

Jeff's car pulled into the driveway just as Lucy pulled back from my embrace.

Lucy said, "Someone is here."

I said, "Oh, that's my brother Jeff, he is all grown up now. He was still a kid when you knew him.

Hey Jeff, do you remember Lucy? She saw me driving home from the store and followed me home."

Jeff said, "I remember Ed talking about you Lucy. Even if I don't remember you I feel like I know you through Ed's conversation about you. You are as lovely as he said you were. Like a spring flower in full bloom. It's God's blessing to you."

Lucy looked at me with astonishment that Jeff would be so bold with his words.

Lucy said, "Glad to meet you Jeff even if you don't remember me, I remember you. You were much younger when your brother and I were together. I always told Ed you were destine for greatness because great people make others feel great, you still have that talent. I hate to run but I have some obligations that just can't wait. This is my home number Ed, give me a call when you want to get together sometime. I'm always home on the weekends."

With that, Lucy was gone, acting like nothing was ever wrong with our relationship. The complexity of the human mind is fascinating to me. Lucy acted as if all the horrible things I did to her never even happened. I, on the other hand, fell deeply in lust with her and could once again lock her in a room as if it was yesterday.

Lucy's life is so messed up that she would settle for the insane relationship we once had. I don't think I need to go there again. As Lucy's car disappeared from sight, I tore up the card with her phone number on it. I just cannot slip back into the darkness of that life. Satan puts the wrong people in your life if you let him.

You cannot be lead by your feelings in this life, Satan can make someone feel very good to be around physically, I know this now. I plan to use the Bible to choose my mate. The words in the Bible will lead me in the right direction.

In 1 Corinthians 6:18-20, it states, 'Flee from sexual immorality. All other sins a person commits are outside the body, but whoever sins sexually, sins against their own body.' I'm done with lust. In my mind, I asked Jesus to help me resist Lucy, and at the name of Jesus the demons trembled, and I was able to tear up the paper with Lucy's phone number. Her lips were pulling me in like a magnet and I could not resist, that's the power of Satan. I know him now and this will never happen to me again.

Jeff said, "How dumb can you get and still breathe, you can't unscramble eggs. I saw you kissing Lucy. How do you think Alice would feel if she was the one pulling into the driveway instead of me?"

I said, "This never happened, you did not see anything. Do you understand?"

Jeff said, "I am not your problem, I don't have loose lips, you know what you did and this is on you Ed. You are the one who has to live with what went on here today."

I said, "Nothing happened other than a kiss. When Lucy knocked on the door, I let her in and immediately realized what could happen and headed for the front porch. I must admit, it was a very powerful kiss but it will never happen again. I've moved on from destructive relationships. I'm looking forward to my future with Alice.

Jeff said, "You know the devil will always test you to see if you will rejoin him. He is very crafty in his ways. He wants you back. He misses you and will do everything in his power to bring you back into his darkness. Once you belonged to him, and he thinks you will get weak enough to fall into your old way of lustfulness, you must show him who you are now. Tell me he doesn't still have a hold on you."

I said, "I must admit Lucy is powerful, with her beauty and sexy nature, I could not resist kissing her. It's like an out of body experience. I just rolled with the flow of her lips. She planted them on me before I had a chance to think about it. When she started to pull back, I pulled her closer and the feelings blocked out the whole world for that moment. I was totally unaware of you driving into the driveway until Lucy pulled away from me. Her lips are like nothing on earth, they take you out of your mind, and it's just like the first time I kissed her. She just does not fade. With most girls the intense feelings lessen, the longer you are with them, but with Lucy every kiss is as intense as the first time you kiss her. Heck, it's been years since I've kissed her and I swear it's stronger than ever. She has been gone for ten minutes and I still have a woody. That is powerful stuff.

Lucy is so screwed up that she liked being locked in a room better than the life she has made for herself. She has all that beauty and no sense to go with it. What a waste.

I will never go down that path again. She led me into a heavy darkness I never knew existed. My body would tremble with depression to the point I thought I was dying; I ceased to exist in my mind. I'm not strong enough to ever dabble in Lucy's darkness again. My life would be destroyed, I'm just not strong enough to go there again and I know it.

That is the new me, thanks to you Jeff. I want the sunshine kind of life. I want love, not lust. I want Alice to take me as high as I can get, I want her to take me to heaven. I've been to hell and I want no part of it again."

Jeff said, "Lucy is so beautiful, how could she be so toxic? I've heard people say that beauty is a curse. The reason it is called a curse is because everyone looks at you and wants to talk to you. They figuratively choke the life out of you, because of how you look. A beautiful person has no peace. Lucy is so gorgeous and magnificent in her looks that when she looked up at me I became paralyzed, helpless and unable to move. My knees became weak and I felt that if I tried to take a step I might fall on my face. That has never happened to me before. It could be because I have never seen such a beautiful creature in real life. Sure, I have seen them on the big screen and on Television, but I've never touched one before. When Lucy reached out her hand to shake mine, it is a good thing she took three steps to meet me because I could not move. When Lucy did touch my hand it was like grabbing an electric bare wire, only it felt good, no pain. It surged through my entire body, head to toe. In case you didn't notice, even I still have a woody. I have absolutely no control over my body. It will just have to go away on its own.

Ed, now I can relate to what you've been trying to tell me. Now that I have seen Lucy, and touched her hand, I confirm, she is electric and even more beautiful than what you described. I know I probably met her before but my memory of her is absent. That bump on the head took a lot out of me."

I said, "She is a beauty but remember to keep her at a distance. The trip is just not worth it. The whole thing turns to pain like you've never felt. Let me spare you from that."

Jeff said, "No need to worry about me, she is interested in you Ed. You are the handsome one in the family; everyone refers to me as cute. That girl is not interested in cute; I can assure you of that. Nature is what it is. I had absolutely no control over the woody she gave me, it finally has gone away."

I said, "Nature is very difficult to control, for a man anyway. I think it's because ours is on the outside. We just give ourselves away when nature calls. We have to wear really long shirts if we want to hide it. Don't feel bad about what happened to you, Lucy has that effect on most all men. Most don't even have to touch her hand, just looking at her is enough.

With Lucy, I had a woody all the time, even when I was too tired to perform. It sounds like heaven but believe you me it was hell; a hell I never want to revisit."

Jeff said, "I'm just glad that I can finally understand what you were talking about when Lucy was the subject. I now understand your weakness when it comes to Lucy. She would be hard to turn down. No girl has ever touched me like that, I was like soft butter in her hand and I think she knew it."

I said, "Oh yes, she knew it. She feels the same thing you feel. I know what I'm talking about, she loves having that power."

Jeff said, "What would you have done if Alice was the one who drove in the driveway instead of me? I already asked you how she would feel about it, now I want to know what you would do."

I said, "That is a good question. No one knows just what they would do, I think I would run and grab Alice and kiss her. I would want Alice to know she is the one for me. I would introduce her to Lucy and explain how Lucy had seen my car and followed me to my home. I would explain that Lucy is the aggressor in this situation and that my heart belongs to Alice and Alice only.

I'm so glad Alice didn't see me, you know it would taint our relationship, women never forget that terrible feeling of being cheated on. Alice must never know of the mistake I made today. It would be so selfish of me to try to clear my conscience by telling her. Besides, nothing like this will ever happen again. Just the thought of hurting Alice repulses me. I should have known better than to even talk to Lucy. I know the effect she has on me. I should have never opened the door. I should have talked to her with the door closed and asked her to leave. I know better than to do what I did today."

Jeff said, "You are right Ed, telling her would only taint your relationship. Why hurt Alice, she doesn't deserve that.

Women seem to compete with each other when it comes to looks, fashion and weight. Alice has the fashion part down pat. Her clothes and hair are spot on with what is trendy, but she lacks in the looks and weight department. If Alice had to compete with Lucy, she couldn't help but feel inadequate. This is only how she would feel because she is everything you could possibly ask for. It would all be in her head, and I want her head to be right, not insecure. Alice is perfect for you Ed, and I want nothing but the best for both of you, therefore what I saw today is between just me and you."

I said, "Thanks little brother, I feel better all ready. Next time the evil one puts beauty in my face I will take off running. I thought that if Lucy was on the front porch I would be safe. You know I would not stay in the living room with her, I'm that smart anyway. If there is a next time, I am taking off, I'm running little brother, do you hear me, running. The evil one will have a hard time catching me. I won't fall for his tricks so easily next time."

Jeff said, "That's half the battle. You must have a plan to escape his clutches. You never know what will happen if you invite evil into your life. You just thought you had the upper hand when you wouldn't let Lucy stay inside your house, she took a piece of you right on the front porch where anyone could see. You got to be smarter than the evil one or he will trip you up."

Little brother is right; if you give the evil one an inch, he will take a mile, that's his game. Alice will never know what happened today, I will protect her from the pain it would cause.

I think I will call her and let her know how much I miss her. Maybe she will let me swing by for an hour.

Chapter 13
Comfort with Alice

Today I did a bad thing. My emotions are all over the place with guilty pleasures from the kiss Lucy planted on my lips. No matter how hard I try to block out the rush that filled my body when her lips touched mine, it just creeps back in. I'm on cloud nine and fighting it all the way. The beautiful Lucy that meant everything to me at one time wants me back in her life. At one time, this would complete my world; I could live in lust and not need another thing. My body would just hum and vibrate in a physical bubble of sexual vibes. It's a whole different level of existence; boundless energy, heightened senses, and a feeling that I owned the world. How long can a body endure all this pleasure before the mind breaks? For me not too long, I have learned this the hard way. I cannot go back there.

Alice will soon be off work and I must see her to keep my sanity. My mind is fragile and my love for Alice will keep me grounded. Lucy keeps trying to creep back into my mind and the struggle to keep her out is making me weak. She is very powerful.

Jeff said, "Ed, I'm going to brew some tea, would you like a cup?"

I said, "Little brother, that's just what I need right now, along with some good conversation about life."

Jeff said, "I don't know how much I can offer in a conversation about life seeing how I've not been in lust or love but I can talk about peace of mind. I prefer the feeling of calm compared to your hyperactive lifestyle. Calm in the mind is where it is at, for me anyway. I like having control of my mind; it makes me feel safe. Of course, my situation with memory loss and all could be a factor in the need for control of my mind and body. What's right for me may not necessarily be right for you. We all have our own little world in our heads. Mine works for me."

I said, "Little brother, you make it all sound so simple. Every time I try to control things, they seem to fall apart, especially when I try to control women. You know little brother, I didn't want Lucy to be in the house because I can't control myself once my feelings take over my body, but she got me anyway on the front porch. Lucy had me melting like hot butter in a pan, with just her lips. That's the only thing that actually touched me.

That may not be true, her beauty touched my eyes and I became soft all over, but her lips melted me instantly, they are what took control anyway. I knew I could not be behind closed doors with Lucy, I did try to control the situation."

Jeff said, "The main reason I try to control my life is because I want only good memories to reflect on when I am old and gray. You know mom and dad always told us that either your memory will give you great pleasures or they will be your nightmares. I never like to dream nightmares. I can't imagine what it would be like to look back on my life, and my life would be a real live nightmare."

I said, "Little brother I want to share with you one of my nightmares that are reoccurring. I am a skeleton and in one eye socket, beautiful women are crawling out. They are crawling out of my mind; they were the death of me. I believe our dreams can be a warning sign if we listen to them."

Jeff said, "I hope you listen and you don't backslide. I would like for you to be in my life until we are old."

Alice should be home from work by now; I must call her and invite her over for dinner. I have two cans of pink salmon and salmon patties would be perfect with asparagus and a salad. I won't even have to go to the store.

Today I let desire overtake reason, how I handle this situation is between God and myself. God is in the center of my life and I always put Him in the center of every room I walk into. This is why I went outside to the porch with Lucy. God is guiding me. No way will I ever let myself be under the influence of Lucy without a good fight. With God on my side, I can win this battle.

You must choose your battles in life wisely. Some people choose to battle a mountain by climbing to the top of it, others choose sports, they strive to be the best on the team, others want to be the best at their job and climb the corporate ladder with their goal to be the top banana, the C.E.O. of the company.

My battle in life is to marry one woman for a lifetime. For better or for worse, in sickness and in health, until death do we part. I want to give my children every tool to make their life a success. When I talk about success, I'm talking about being able to relate to other people and learning about relationships that are healthy. This is what children learn at a very early age by watching mommy and daddy. This has to be learned at home, you don't learn this in a school book. Alice is the woman that I want to make a family with, until death do we part. You cannot rewind your life, going forward it will be Alice, our future family, and me. Lucy is in the past and that is where she is staying.

Alice is on her way and I am so excited. I will have a quick shower to clear my head and a close shave for Alice to stroke my cheek.

The doorbell rang, and when I opened the door, there

stood Alice more beautiful than ever. I stood in the doorway just drinking in her presence.

Alice said, "Well are you going to invite me in or just stand there and stare?"

I said, "Of course, come right in. You just take me over the moon every time I see you. It takes a minute for me to get grounded."

Alice said, "Is everything okay? You sounded desperate on the phone, like something is wrong."

I said, "I must admit I really wanted to spend some time with you. Can I kiss you Alice?"

Alice said, "I thought you would never ask."

I grabbed Alice, tilted her chin back, studied her face, and when she began to melt into my arms I placed my lips on hers; all the pent up energy in my body was being consumed by Alice. Never in my life have I felt such pleasure from a kiss. By the time our lips were parting, I became numb. The body can only stand so much pleasure before it goes limp.

Alice said, "You are in my blood and pulsing through my entire body; you are my heartbeat. Can we go into your room and lay together for a while?"

I said, "That's not a good idea, we are not married yet. I don't want to put us in a compromising position to jeopardize our relationship. You haven't even told me that you love me. I will never lay with a woman who doesn't love me. That kind of behavior is all in the past for me. I will only settle for the real deal, now that my eyes are open."

Alice said, "I'm falling head over hills for you. That word you want to hear I have never told to a man that I have dated. Only family members have heard me say that word. I don't even know if I can say it even if I feel it. It's different in the meaning with a man. It is a commitment that you cannot go back on. For me it is not the kind of thing that will go away and I will say to the next guy I date. It will have real lasting meaning when I say it. He will become part of the family."

I said, "I want to be a family member and if you think I will fit, you just let me know."

About that time, Jeff came around the corner, nodded his head and smiled. I was still holding Alice in my arms and I know Jeff had to feel awkward.

Alice said, "Hello Jeff, I didn't know you were even in the house."

Jeff said, "Hello Alice, I didn't mean to interrupt you two. I was just going to help with the salmon patties. I wanted to show how I could open the can since you showed me your trick with the oil. Come here Alice and watch."

Alice said, "It's much better than the last time I saw you struggling to open a can. Another little trick is to hold the can up off the table just about one-eighth of an inch, kind of like the electric can openers have the can in the air. It will open twice as fast."

Jeff said, "You are right, it just glides. Thanks for the tip Alice."

I'm just gazing at Alice as Jeff and her cut up with each other. Alice is going to fit in perfect with my family; I can't wait for the rest of them to meet her.

Dinner tasted better than ever, partly because Alice was at the table sharing conversation with us and partly because Alice added some spices and onions in the salmon patties.

Jeff headed out the door to visit a friend and now it is just the two of us. Together we clear the table and wash the dishes. Every time I brush up against Alice I feel a spark, the look on Alice's face tells me she is feeling the same thing.

After the kitchen is cleaned, we head to the living room for some relaxation. The mood of the room is heading back to where it was when Alice asked if we could lay in my bed together.

I said, "Alice, will you marry me? I'm so in love

with you I can hardly function when you are not around. I want you to be in my life as a wife."

Alice said, "I need time to be sure this is not just a phase you are going through and you wake up and realize you can do much better than me."

I said, "Whatever you say Alice. I don't care if we wait ten years and then marry, I just want you to be with me every day. In ten years, I will be thirty-seven years old but still young enough to start a family with at least three children. You see Alice, I've never met a woman that I wanted to have children with. You are the only woman who has ever made me realize how great life can be when you are making a family. I think about what great parents we will be and the love that our family will share with each other."

Alice said, "I don't know that I want to wait ten years to find out if we are right for each other or not, but I do need some time. You see Ed, I'm in lust with you. You make the chemicals in my brain do cartwheels. I want to take you in the other room right now and experience sex with you in every position known to mankind. I want to do anything you want me to do.

That other word you keep talking about, love, means taking a chance of getting my heart broke. It involves my mind. I've seen people with broken minds and seldom do they recover. Before I take a chance on a broken heart, I must be sure we are the real thing that can last the test of time.

I already have a handicap because I'm ugly, it took years to feel good about myself, for something to matter other than the way I look. I got my education and a great job as an accountant. Those things gave me the confidence to feel equal in life with normal people. I've always felt like a freak. In my young life, kids would make fun of me because I was fat and ugly. It scarred my mind and to this day it creeps into my life and I begin to feel insecure about myself.

I'm not trying to get you to feel sorry for me, I just want you to understand why I need to be slow about handing my heart over to you. It takes years for me to recover from pain in the brain."

I said, "For certain, you are the most beautiful woman I've ever known, Alice you must accept that. You can rest at ease that I will never leave you or hurt you on purpose. If I ever hurt you, it will be because I'm unaware of what causes you pain. If that happens we will talk about it and I promise, it will never happen again.

You take all the time you need Alice, I'm not trying to rush you into anything, I just want you to know how in love with you I am. If anyone gets hurt in this relationship, it will be me. Alice, pain is pain and beautiful people feel pain just as deep as anyone else does in this world. Actually, the people in the middle who look ordinary have less mental pain than those whose looks go in the extreme.

You will always be my beautiful Alice and I will never leave you. Please believe me."

Alice said, "I know you believe what you are saying right now and when my mind gives in to take a chance on you, I will give you my all."

My mind is in a good place now. I have control of my emotions and two women tested me today. A year ago I would have given into both of them in the same day.

I'm so excited that Alice wants to spend more time with me. It doesn't matter what we do, I am never bored when Alice is with me. We could be as poor as a church mouse and feel like we were the richest people on earth. That is what Alice's presence does to me.

Alice has a problem saying the word 'love,' and if she never tells me she loves me, it will be just fine with me, as long as she is with me. Being together for the rest of our lives is all that matters to me. Even if she wants to take the word love out of our marriage ceremony, I will not complain. All I want Alice to do is to promise she will be with me until I die, that's all I want.

Chapter 14
Soul Searching

All I can think about is Alice, and what makes her tick. If she is to become my lifetime partner, I have to find a way to make her want to marry me.

I understand why I had problems with women in the past, but everything about me is different now. I am capable of real love and want to have children with Alice and to be a family. This is what God wants for His children and I must ask for His guidance and search for answers in His book, the Bible. The Bible is my foundation that I always go back to.

2 Timothy 1:6-7 states, "For God has not given us a spirit of fear, but of power and of love and of a sound mind." Through God's guidance, I now have a sound mind, love in my heart for Alice, and I have achieved the power to say no to lovely women. I have it all except a marriage license with Alice's name on it.

Being with God lights me up on the inside. This light burns brighter when Alice is with me. My love for Alice goes beyond just physical feelings, it is as if we are both in this higher existence, God's light is upon us. We are meant to be married to each other.

Alice was not raised to believe in God yet she searches for answers of her existence. In my heart, I know she will find God. I know this because she questions the way her parents raised her. Reading the Bible will give Alice the answers she is looking for, and she reads it daily.

Alice is a good person and I have always said that your actions define who you are. God will be happy for Alice to join His team. She stands for everything God wants us to value. She just needs to be introduced to Him, by reading His words from the beginning to the end she will find her answer, God's world is where she belongs.

I wonder if I should slow it down with Alice and me. It is possible that I'm smothering her when I'm with her and she is unable to think and realize how much I love her. Maybe she feels like a prisoner of my love. I'm so wowed by her presence every time we are together that I just have to be as close to her as possible. My body becomes filled with her presence and I know she can feel my need to be near her. If I slow it down just a tad and let her become the aggressor, she will pursue me and she will be the one asking to marry me.

I know Alice is in love with me, I can feel her love travel through my body every time she touches me. I just need to find a way to get her to admit that I am the one for her, that she feels safe with me, for I will never hurt her.

Alice has told me that she has seen people destroyed by love, their minds broke along with their heart, and they were never the same. My love for Alice is so strong that I can see where she could be afraid of the depth it could take her. At times, my love is so deep that there is a fine line between the bliss and darkness. It can be a dark deep lust and love all wrapped up together. No other woman has taken me to this place and it truly scares me at times. When I go there, I can see in Alice's eyes that she feels it as well. It is as if we could drop off the edge of sanity.

Alice need not worry for I will never break her mind or heart. Her well-being will always be at the top of my list. She is safe with me, I know how far to go with my love for Alice.

I have been through many destructive relationships and all that is behind me. Lucy proved to me that I don't need that in my life anymore. Lucy is just one of the ten women that winded up in a very dark place with me. I have lost my mind with each of these women, these beautiful creatures that I put in a cage like a zoo animal. I know what I did to each of them and I feel horrible about being a monster and causing pain.

Right now, my biggest fear is that Alice is in lust with me and not in love with me. I want her to have both lust and love. A relationship cannot exist without both, not for a lifetime anyway. Alice only having lust for me scares me. That would be the ultimate payback for every heart I ever broke.

When I say I'm going to give Alice some room I'm talking about not hovering around her and sitting so close you couldn't put a finger between us. I want to be with her every day; I just won't smother her anymore.

When Alice was helping Jeff with the salmon patties, and I observed at a distance, I derived great pleasure watching the two of them converse. Anything Alice does give's me great pleasure. Just being in the same room with her is enough for me.

My fear is that Alice is morphing into the old me, nothing but sex on the mind. She is not the least bit shy about sharing her mind with me sexually. What she doesn't know is that she will never have me that way unless she marries me. She seems to think I will get weak and give in because I'm a guy. She has no idea how strong I am about getting my way on this issue. Alice is about to find out I mean what I say when I say no.

The only way Alice can lose me is if I die. These conjured up fears that I will break her heart is just her imagination. No one wants a broken heart but to hear Alice express her fear you would think I was going to run over her with a Mack truck. What I would do to her would be worse than any heartbreak in the history of all heartbreaks.

If I have to take her to counseling to get this out of her head, I am willing to do that. I will even let them council me with Alice, anything to make things the best for the two of us. I'm totally open to any insight that will wash away Alice's fear. I just want a relationship that will last a lifetime, and be the best thing to ever happen to her.

If indeed giving Alice room to breathe works, I will have to control my passion for Alice and give her all the room she needs even after we are married. I may be the one who needs to change. I may be as much of the problem as Alice is.

What goes up must come down is an old saying that has a lot of meaning to it. Drugs took me over the moon and took me to the bottom of hell itself. Love changes the chemicals in your body naturally that can take you over the moon. Many people are addicted to the natural feelings that love brings into their life, which is healthy as long as they are not changing partners all the time. That was my mistake. As soon as I started to come down or I thought my partner at the time was coming down, I either changed partners or locked up the woman that was coming down from loves high.

Now that I have had a ton of experience with life, I can see all the mistakes that come with relationships. The biggest mistake is trying to change your partner. You must adjust yourself to the circumstances. If the circumstances are more than you can bear, this is not the right life partner for you. Enjoy their company but lock up your heart and save it for the right person.

I know the right person for me is Alice and I'm willing to do anything for a lifelong relationship with her.

If I can control my passion when I'm with Alice, and unleash it when she feels strong enough to handle it, she might just feel safe enough to let down her guard.

I'm going to adjust to the circumstances that will make Alice feel comfortable and if she is comfortable, she can't help falling in love with me.

That will be my strategy. I will tone things down to the level that normal people live their whole life. The problem I have created for myself is that I put myself out there without any restraints. Alice has seen the whole package that I have to offer except for sex. If we have sex, she will have nothing left to explore. This must be why she keeps asking to have sex with me. She wants to know every detail about me, when she does all the mystery will be out of our relationship. That's just not going to happen. Alice will have to marry me before she gets anything more than a kiss from me. If restraint is what it takes to win Alice's love then I'm willing to chain my emotions to the ground. If a normal relationship is what it takes to win Alice's love then I can be normal. It may be just what she needs. All my excitement will still be in my head, I just won't throw up my excitement all over Alice. I will keep all my butterflies in my stomach.

It is possible that I am a sex object to Alice, and she wants to gratify her feelings of lust and she feels no love in her heart for me. I'm not the first person that has happened to. Many women had that experience with me. They were just sex objects and when I tired of them, I traded them off for another pretty face. I never felt anything more than lust for any of them.

If Alice feels this way toward me, I will have to accept my fate. I will have to be man enough to walk away and continue my search for my lifelong mate.

Chapter 15
Heart to Heart Talk

It's time to find out if I'm wasting my time waiting for Alice to marry me. I need to know if she is just stringing me along, thinking I will give in and be her sex toy, or will I be her husband?

I admit that I have lust in my heart for Alice, but it is in combination with an overpowering love as well. I need Alice to tell me if she also has both, or if I'm only seen as a sex object. I have to know what is in Alice's heart.

Jeff is spending the evening with a friend so I have the place to myself. I invited Alice over for dinner and told her we needed to talk things over.

The doorbell is ringing and my body fills with a state of panic. Confronting Alice may just be the beginning of the end of our relationship. I have to take that chance, rather than waste our time on a 'going nowhere relationship.'

I said, "Come in Alice, you look stunning tonight, strikingly attractive. You take my breath away."

Alice said, "Oh Ed, you always say the right words to excite my soul. When you talk I just perk up all over."

We are off to a good start feeling each other's excitement, gazing into each other's eyes and getting lost in the moment.

I have prepared grilled salmon with lime juice on the side to enhance the flavor, sweet potatoes with a pad of butter, and a five-leaf salad with sliced strawberries on top.

I pull a chair out for Alice to sit, I kiss her cheek. I cannot help myself. I want Alice to have a clear head when we talk but I fuzzy it up with a kiss on the cheek. I may be more of a problem than a solution. How can Alice think straight when I'm pouring my feelings all over her?

Alice said, "I love your brother Jeff but it's nice to spend time in your home with just you and me.

This salmon is delicious, I'm so impressed that you cooked this meal for me, and this salad is so nutritious with baby kale and strawberries. It is my favorite combination. Everything about you is so perfect."

I said, "I'm so far from perfect that when you say that it scares me that I could never live up to what you image me to be. One day your eyes will open to what a screw-up I am and you will take off running."

Alice said, "Nobody is perfect, I'm just saying you are perfect for me, I can take your screw-ups and even enjoy them."

Well things are off to a great start tonight, Alice knows I'm not perfect, and is willing to accept that part of me. There is a comfortable silence at the dinner table as we eat and glance at each other occasionally.

Alice said, "Ed, you don't have any pets do you, like animals?"

I said, "I love animals, I think they are delicious."

Alice laughed a hardy deep down belly laugh, as we looked deep into each other's eyes. Laughter is a shared feeling that is bringing us closer in a deeper sort of way.

Alice said, "I agree, animals are delicious but what I meant was do you have any pets?"

I said, "I raised a cow from a baby because his mother rejected him, and one day when he was about five-hundred pounds, he was showing me some affection and pinned me to my truck by rubbing up against me. I thought I would die right there because he squeezed the breath right out of me. I could not holler or anything, I was dying when my dad noticed and pulled the cow off me. I fell to the ground and my lungs ached, I struggled to fill them with air once again. I thought I was dying. I have not had a pet since then."

Alice said, "That is the funniest story I have ever heard."

I could have sworn that I told her that story before, but it's the kind of story that is always funny, even if you have heard it before.

We are having a great time so I will wait until later to get serious about our future.

Alice said, "I see why you don't have any pets now. Did you know that a meat-eaters diet is responsible for more than seven times as much greenhouse-gas emissions as a vegan's diet is? When I found this out I started eating only vegetables, two days a week.

I want to do my part in saving the planet. When the hybrid cars are less expensive I plan to purchase one of them also."

I said, "That's great that you are concerned with the planet Alice, so am I.

Did you know that switching from a standard meat eating diet to a complete vegetarian diet is more effective than trading your gas car in for a hybrid?"

Alice said, "Don't put me on a guilt trip. I have no intentions of giving up meat completely. I just said I want to make a small difference. If everyone did what I'm doing, the world would be a better place. That's all I'm saying, everyone needs to vegan at least twice a week. I still want to enjoy my meat."

I said, "My biggest fear for our planet is drinking water. With all the chemicals, we contaminate the ground with; they can't help but get into our water system, what if we can't filter all of them out?

Our body is 84% water, that's a lot. Our muscles are 76% water and our bones are 22% water. We can't exist without large amounts of water and our body will not function properly without it.

What I do is use environmental friendly soap. It cost a little more but it's worth it to me."

Alice said, "We have so much in common. I'm amazed when I find out these things about us. How about I change to your soap and you go vegan two days a week?"

I said, "That sounds doable to me. We can both feel better about ourselves and what we are doing for our planet."

Alice said, "Now that we are committed to making our planet healthier, what do you recommend for the people walking on it to be happy?"

I said, "That's an easy question to answer. It all starts whey you are young. The greatest gift we can give our children is a great marriage. We must show them how to live. My parents gave me that and my childhood was amazing. Things went bad for me when I moved out on my own and started dating and running around with the beautiful people. They live in a very fast world. My parents are average looking people so they never fell in with the beautiful people and did not know how to teach me about that world. Because I had a good foundation from my parents, I was able to rise above my mistakes. Being dangerously handsome has its pitfalls; it takes an emotional toll on the mind.

I like how the Bible tells us how to raise our children. In Deuteronomy 6:6-7 it states, 'And these words, which I command thee this day, shall be in thy heart: And thou shalt teach them diligently onto thy children, and shalt talk of them when thou sittest in thine house, and when thou walkest by the way, and when thou liest down and when thou risest up.'

You must raise your children to know right from wrong, it is your duty, this is how the world will find happiness."

Alice said, "You know I've been reading the Bible and that very passage got my attention. We are responsible for teaching our children how to live. It's my opinion that teaching them to be respectful of others will take them a long way in this world we live in. They must know people are different, each culture has its own set of values and it is up to each of us to learn what they are. Understanding leads to respect. If I have children, they will have a clear understanding of why people are the way they are.

Every one always says people should stay off the subjects of religion and politics but I disagree. Those two subjects are probably the most eye opening subjects of a person's values. You can get a true picture of the nature a person has and you will be able to avoid touchy subjects that lead to conflict.

I like the way you dance all around religion, yet you never try to make me feel guilty because I have a different view. I wonder if we can touch on politics without looking at each other differently."

I said, "I hope we have the ability to grow into the best we can be our entire life. This means we can change our political views as long as it is in a positive way for our planet and ourselves. Things change in this world and we must be flexible to roll with what is best for our country. We are lucky enough to live in the richest and most powerful country in the world; I believe it to be the promise land that the Bible talks about. If we are to remain in the land of milk and honey, we must protect the moral value this country was founded on.

That says it all in a nutshell, I see no reason to address a particular subject of conflict. I have a right to believe what I want to believe just as every American has the right to believe what they want to believe. It's the laws we have to obey and the only way to change the laws is with the officials we elect into office. We vote for who will represent our views and this is how our country works. We have the freedom to believe and express our views as long as it is not breaking any laws."

Alice said, "We have some of the same views on politics and for me in a nutshell is the word freedom. That word says it all. Freedom is the most important thing this country has, and we must protect it with every means possible, with the people we put in office. I like the fact that we both recognize what a great country we live in. You know Ed; most people take our country for granted. Most do not even vote, and give lame excuses like, 'I'm just one vote, what difference can I make?' The truth is that they are too selfish to take the time to vote. If they don't wake up, one day they could lose it all, by all, I mean their freedoms. We could become a third world country overnight."

Things are going in the right direction. Alice is talking about her views, in a somewhat guarded way but at least she is talking. She has however, avoided saying whether she would teach the Bible to her children. I'm going to brave it and just ask her.

I said, "Alice, how do you feel about raising your children to attend church and learn about God?"

Alice said, "I would be open to teaching my children about God, and if the man I marry is active in a church, he could take them to church. Who knows, by the time I'm done reading the Bible, I may start going to church myself.

Right now, I'm reading the book of Daniel. I'm drawn to the words in Daniel 2:21-22 'And he changeth the times and the seasons: he removeth kings, and setteth up kings: he giveth wisdom unto the wise, and knowledge to them that know understanding:22He revealeth the deep and secret things: he knoweth what is in the darkness, and the light dwelleth with him.'

I like the part where he gives knowledge to them that know understanding. I think by having the gift of understanding we can reach people and help them in difficult times. If we can't actually help them ourselves, we can tell them where to get help. I have a good friend that continually pushes her self-destruct button. I'm no doctor but I was able to get her to see a doctor to help her deal with her impulses. She has learned in the business world to restrain herself from falling for every man who makes a move on her. She is very successful now and has cleaned up her image as far as mixing it up with others in the office. She can't help it if she is attractive and men are drawn to her. She now has the tools of knowledge to deal with the situation. She knows to say, 'This is inappropriate behavior, please stop.' This worked for her and restored her reputation.

My friend was walking in darkness but with knowledge of how to handle herself, she is walking in the light of success.

The Bible is full of stories that fit right into modern times, even though it was wrote thousands of years ago. People who live by the Bible will be spared all the drama that wrong behavior can brings into their life.

The answer to your questions is that I would tell my children that church and learning about God could teach them how to live a charmed life. I would encourage them to read the Bible. It could very well be the greatest Book ever written."

I said, "That's encouraging. If they read about God in the Bible they will learn my secret to happiness, you let God control your life, not yourself. That's when I fell into happiness. I asked God for forgiveness for all my sins that God is aware of, even if I'm not aware of everything I've done. I want my children to know that God forgives everything and He loves them like He loves His only Son."

Alice said, "I'm glad you found God. That guy you used to be sounded selfish, like he was running with the devil.

According to the Bible, the devil has us choose misery over joy and bondage over freedom, the devil is the father of all lies, he is the master of lies.

For me, the secret to happiness is simple. It's not where you go or what you do that makes you happy, it's who you are with that makes you happy. If you are by yourself, you better like yourself, and if you are with another, you better like them. Happiness is a state of mind and everything is better if your mind is right.

I totally agree with you on the part that if you don't repent you will be empty inside. Everyone messes up in life, the secret is to make that wrong a right."

I said, "We are so much alike in our thinking. We read each other like we grew up together or something. I like the fact that we accept each other the way we are. We can express our feelings without trying to change each other's minds. I like that we have an unspoken goodness for each other. We don't need constant acknowledgement of our actions, whether they be good or bad.

Alice, I asked you here tonight because I need to know what is in your heart for our future. I know you are as attracted to me as I am to you. I need to know if your feelings are only physical. Do you see us sharing our life as one or are you just having a good time?"

Alice said, "You are really putting me on the spot right now. I've never seen you so serious. You are scaring me. Will you lighten up."

Alice left the table and started looking through the CD's for some music to play. She is avoiding my question.

I approach her from behind and place my hands on her shoulders. Alice turns slowly and our lips gently meet. Suddenly I'm in a haze and nothing matters but Alice's lips on mine. We are both trembling with excitement and hunger for each other. My passion is uncontrollable as my hands rub all over Alice's back.

Alice said, "Can we go into the bedroom so we can lie down?"

I pulled back and came to my senses. Lust will not dominate this relationship; we have more than that going for us. I must make Alice see further down the road, to a lasting marriage.

I refuse to answer Alice's question, 'can we go into the bedroom?' I grab Alice's glass and go into the kitchen to freshen her drink with more ice.

Alice said, "Do you like Jazz? I'm in the mood for Jazz. You know the music you like is an expression of yourself. Jazz gets me all jazzed up and excited about life."

When I sat Alice's drink down she grabbed me and we started dancing to a slow jazz tune that lightened my mood. Alice starts kissing my neck lightly. Chills are going up and down my spine as Alice finds my lips once again. It's as if my body is lighting up as Alice kisses me, it's getting brighter and brighter.

I said, "To feel your breath on my face is to feel your soul on my face. My heart is like wax melting from your breath. I'm so jazzed right now I can't think straight. Alice your eyes sing a sweet melody of love, do you love me Alice?"

Alice pulled back and the moment was lost. Alice became panicky. She sat on the couch and turned her head away from me.

Alice said, "I don't know what love is. How can I answer a question like that if I don't even know what it is? I've never told anyone but my parents that I love them. All my relationships with men are short and sweet, no lasting relationships. No real pain like I've seen my friends go through. I've experienced enough pain in life just because of the way I look. I don't want the kind of lifelong pain that comes with lost love. I personally know a ninety-year-old woman who still talks about her first love and all the pain that went with it, when he left her. I can't possibly keep you for a lifetime. One day you will wake up; and see me for what I am, a troll."

I said, "Don't you ever talk about yourself like that again. You are the most beautiful person inside and out that I've ever known. You hurt me deeply when you talk like that."

Alice said, "You make me feel beautiful but I know what people think when they see me. It's even more pronounced when I'm with you. It's like I can read their minds, 'What is he doing with that?' Let me finish before you give me a hard time, you need to know what is going on in my mind. I know you can't possibly understand how I feel, because you are drop dead gorgeous, but you must understand my insecurities when it comes to my future and how hard it is to let my feelings grow into what you want."

I said, "Alice, I only know what I see and it is you, the mother of my children and the person I want to grow old with. You are all I want in life."

Alice said, "I need time to be sure you don't come to your senses before I even think about giving you my heart."

I said, "I assure you Alice, you are the only woman for me. If you leave me, I will be like that ninety-year-old woman talking about her first love. You see Alice, I've never been in love. You are my first and only love. There is no need to wait; no woman on earth will ever take your place. Please Alice, if you can fall in love with me, let yourself fall head over hills for me.

If you know you will never love me, please just tell

me and move on with your life.

All I ask is that you let yourself know without a doubt that I will always cherish and love you no matter what the outcome."

Alice said, "I have a great desire inside my body to be with you. I want to feel your body against mine with all the romance ever known to mankind, but I don't know if it is just lust. I just don't know what I'm feeling. Can my lust grow into love?"

I said, "I cannot fill your lustful need until we are married. We must have love and lust all wrapped up together. I won't settle for anything less."

Alice just looked at me like she was lost for the right words. At least tonight, I realize the insecurities Alice faces in our relationship. All her fear is superficial. It's all an outward thing, nothing that really matters inside the heart. I think we can conquer these fears that plague Alice.

It's possible that it's my fault for acknowledging beautiful women's advances towards me when Alice is with me. Maybe the nod of my head or the wink of my eye or just the hello to another woman in Alice's presence is what makes Alice think she is not the only one in my mind.

I look at beautiful women as a fresh-bloomed flower or a beautiful piece of artwork; gifts from God to make our world a pleasant place to live and enjoy. Alice on the other hand may perceive these beautiful creatures as a threat that will eventually steal her handsome boyfriend from her, causing her great pain and regret.

All of Alice's problems with a lifetime commitment could be caused by my actions when we are out and about. I'm the one who needs to change.

Chapter 16
Changes

Being flattered by Lucy's advances could cost me the love of my life, Alice. It is possible that I'm so consumed with making myself feel good by being noticed, that I have put in jeopardy what is meant to be, my future life with Alice. Kissing Lucy back will never happen again. Even though it has been a while back that this happened, it is fresh on my mind.

I thought I learned my lesson about being selfish. For me selfishness led to a deep dark depression with no light at the end of the tunnel. It took an intervention with family and friends to pull me back into the light of happiness. I can't dip back into that dark place again because of my selfish nature. I refuse to be the reason why I lose Alice. I know I could never be happy again if my actions pushed Alice out of my life. I'm making changes today. Alice is the only girl for me and I'm making the changes without saying a word to Alice about my plan. After all, actions speak louder than words.

Tonight I'm taking Alice to the horse races and we are having dinner on the third floor while we watch. I'm going to be aware of my actions and Alice is going to know that she is the only woman for me, now and forever. Alice is going to know that my selfish nature, is going to be a thing of the past. I don't want depression in my life anymore and selfish people have more problems with depression than normal people. I'm going to prove to myself tonight that Alice is the only person for me and she is going to know that also tonight. My past actions are not part of our future.

The first thing I'm going to do is buy Alice a long scarf to wrap around her neck with a large floppy hat to match. The Kentucky Derby will be broadcast on the big screen before the actual live derby starts. Everyone dresses up for this occasion. I like Alice in white, so that will be the color I choose. After all, white goes with any color of dress that Alice will wear.

I asked the clerk to wrap the present extra fancy; I wanted to wow Alice when she opens the door. The clerk curled the ribbons and by the time she was done, the present was pretty enough to wear as a hat itself.

As I'm walking towards Alice's front door, out of the corner of my eye, I catch someone looking out the window. I wave, and before I had a chance to ring the bell, Alice opened the door.

Alice said, "Is that beautiful package for me?"

I said, "You and only you my sweet Alice."

I kissed her on the cheek and she blushed, the prettiest pink that matched her pink dress. Alice marveled at the perfectly wrapped gift and sat it on the table. She took her camera and snapped a quick shot of the gift before opening it. I'm glad she did, it let me know that she noticed how perfect it looked to her.

Alice said, "Oh Ed, this is the most beautiful hat and scarf I've ever seen. Let me put it on and model it for you. Will you take a picture of me? I may never look this fancy again. I want to remember this moment."

Alice is so excited that it makes my heart sing with pleasure. I want to make her this happy every day of her life.

I said, "You wear it well. I think it was made just for you."

Alice said, "I will feel like I'm at the Kentucky Derby. I doubt anyone there will have a prettier hat and scarf than mine. Thank you so much Ed. This is the best present anyone has ever given me."

Alice began walking towards me, one foot directly in front of the other, like a model on the runway. Just as she was right in front of me, she turned on her heels and walked the other way. As she reached the other side of the room, she slowly turned her head over her right shoulder and looked me up and down. Our eyes locked and her body made a full turn and we began walking towards each other. No words are necessary at this time as we melt into each other's arms. Alice's lips gentle and cautiously are upon my lips with a sweetness I've never tasted in my life. That's right, sweetness, not lustfulness. Our relationship is reaching a higher plateau then I've ever experienced in my life. No woman has ever made me feel the way Alice does in this blissful moment. I'm in paradise.

Alice said, "Let me grab my purse and sunglasses and we can be on our way."

She left me standing there in a daze of sweetness like she hadn't done anything at all. I don't want to snap out of this feeling so I hold on to the moment as long as I can. It is like my entire body is glowing, that is how strong this feeling is, and I imagine heaven must be a lot like I feel right now. If I had wings, I would be flying right now.

Alice grabs my hand and pulls me out the door before the spell is broken. Alice locks the door and we are off to the races.

As I'm driving, I remind myself of a passage in the Bible, Matthew 5:27-28, 'Ye have heard that it was said by them of old time, Thou shalt not commit adultery: But I say onto you, that whosoever looketh on a woman to lust after her hath committed adultery with her already in his heart.'

I have sinned and I own it, I get it now, my sin of

looking at beautiful women with lust made Alice insecure in our relationship.

Most people say they made a mistake, but instead of that word I use, I sinned. A mistake is something you make on an English test. Lust is bigger than a mistake, it's on purpose.

I'm such a jerk to have ever let my eyes fall on another woman while in the presence of Alice. Tonight I will prove to myself that my past behavior is in the past. My eyes will be on the love of my life, Alice.

As we enter the race track there was a substance in the air called excitement. This is a very big day for the horses and trainers; both have the chance to show off their talents. The two of them will be responsible for the outcome; they are the ones doing all the work, they have been preparing for weeks leading up to this day.

I place my hand in the small of Alice's back and guide her through the crowd in the direction of the elevators. We ride to the third floor, and as we exit sure enough, there is a beautiful woman right in front of us and she has eyes for me. I'm not looking at her but I can feel her eyes and so can Alice. I refuse to acknowledge her existence so she approaches us and asks, "Don't I know you?" She pretended to be addressing both of us as I looked the other way, and Alice asked me if I knew the lady standing in front of us. I let her know that I have never seen her before in my life. Alice told the lady that she must be mistaken and we proceeded to our dinner table. It felt so good to know the strength I just showed.

I always thought of abuse as striking a woman, which I would never do, but it goes deeper than that. Locking a woman up where she can't be with other people is a form of abuse and flirting with other women whey you are with someone is a form of abuse. I'm done with both forms of abuse. They are nothing but selfish gratification and I'm done with that. I want happiness, not gratification.

Alice said, "Are you sure you don't know that woman? She was looking at you more than at me."

I said, "All she wanted was to enter our world, I've never seen her before in my life. That was just a line she was using."

Alice perked up and adjusted her hat as if she had just won a race herself. A big smile came across her face, and she began to order a steak, medium-rare, with a baked potato and a glass of wine. I told the waiter, "I'll have the same, only with a glass of rain, you know water." We all started laughing and the waiter said he would be right back with our drinks.

The racetrack is full of beautiful people so I have my work cut out for me tonight. Across the room is a table with three women who kept staring at our table.

Alice said, "Do you know those women at the table near the window?"

I said, "Never seen them before in my life. They must be admiring your hat. Why don't you smile and tip your hat at them."

Alice did just what I suggested her to do and they smiled back and turned away.

Alice is in control of the evening and I can see the confidence all over her face. She is beaming. I have a stirring in my heart, it is God, no more toxic relationships for me. I'm living a story worth telling. I have to run from things I know are wrong for me. Alice is my second chance in life and I'm not messing that up. A force beyond myself, the Bible, guides me. God did surgery on my brain tonight and made me whole, with His word. We become what we worship, I worship God, and I want to be like God. He is transforming my way of thinking and it is making Alice and me so happy tonight.

The waiter brought our food and drinks, and asked if we needed anything else. We both let him know we were happy with the way our dinners looked. The waiter asked if the house dressing was okay for our salads, we both nodded yes. He placed it in the center of the table and was off to attend another customer.

Alice said, "This dinner is delicious, the wine has a perfect dry flavor, I just love it."

I wish she could use the love word for our relationship, like 'I love you Ed.', that would be music to my ears.

I said, "Look Alice, they are loading the horses; it is time for the first race. I like number five, that big brown horse with the black tail."

Alice said, "So do I, he looks like a strong one, let's root for him to win."

The Thoroughbred horses are beautiful tonight. The one we like looks more like an Arabian stallion. Thoroughbred horses are a cross of Arabian stallions with English mares. They are bred of pure stock so they can run distances of a mile or more. This race is for a mile and a quarter.

The bell rang and the horses are off to a fast start. The jockey riding the number five horse is wearing yellow, and that is how we are keeping up with him.

Number five is moving to the outside so he doesn't have to eat the dirt from the horses in front of him. Smart move. He is passing one horse after another and Alice is beginning to root for him out loud. Her eyes are getting glassy with excitement as she stands and starts yelling for number five to win. Just as he crosses the finish line, Alice takes off her hat and swirls it in the air saying, 'That's what I'm talking about.'

Alice puts her hat back on and gently sits down like a lady. She is all smiles.

Alice said, "That was so exciting I lost all control when number five started passing all the other horses. Can you believe we picked a winner? Well, you picked a winner; I just went along with you. I figured a country boy would know a thing or two about a horse. Tell me Ed, how did you do that?"

I said, "It was good judgment and good luck. All

these horses are well bred; I just liked the way the number five horse looked like an Arabian horse with that small head.

You really got excited, I'm glad he won for us, even though we didn't bet on him. I never bet. I just like watching them run. They are very competitive and fun to watch."

Alice said, "I'll say, you are spot on. My heart was beating as fast as those horses were running. I can only imagine what it is like for the horses and the jockeys on that track. What an exciting life they are living."

We are having the perfect evening. Alice is feeling comfortable in her own skin. Tonight she is the most beautiful woman in the room and it shows by the way that she is handling herself, with confidence.

Love is to bring your mate to a higher level for the good of the relationship. Alice has reached that level because my eyes tonight are only on her.

I can feel the eyes of beautiful women on me but I don't look into their eyes so I can feel the rush it brings, my eyes are only on Alice and she knows that. This may be just what Alice needed, my individual attention.

Tonight I'm flirting with Alice only. Flirting is all about being spontaneous and as we were leaving the racetrack, I grabbed Alice and kissed her right in front of everyone. With my lips on Alice's lips, everything became a haze and it was as if we were the only people on earth for that moment. As our lips parted Alice said, "I've transitioned into the sexiest girl in the building tonight," and I said, "Indeed you are."

We walked on cloud nine to our car without another word, only holding hands with electric charges going through our bodies. Alice is capable of loving me; I just need her to tell me.

Chapter 17
Spirit of Wisdom

I have reached a higher plateau by being wise with my actions. Sometimes it is a mystery to me, why it took me this long to figure out how to ease Alice's mind about our relationship. I've put my selfish way of needing to be noticed, and enjoying it, in front of Alice. How could I be so insensitive to her feelings?

The games the beautiful people play, by always looking at one another for a buzz, can't be applied when it is not a level playing field. My eyes are open to the pain I caused Alice, and all that is behind me now. I tried to bring Alice into my ego driven world where she didn't belong, I don't belong there anymore either. I have no use for that shallow world of only temporary feelings that fade from one person into another. The feelings are all lust based and leave you empty feeling in the end. They are only instant gratification and once you get to know the person, most of the time you don't even like them. Sure, they are something for the eye to behold, but the regrets are not worth the rush for me anymore. Alice is my non-stop rush. She is the only woman my eyes want to see for the rest of my life. I want a real life with a family that loves me, children from Alice that I will treasure and share myself with. I want to make my family the center of my life. I want to play ball with my children, take them to movies and on a vacation once a year, I want to be a big part of their life. I want to breathe the breath of love into my family and have them feel it.

We have control of our actions and we are responsible for how our family turns out. A person can live in the ghetto but not be ghetto. If children are provided the love and guidance from their parents, they can rise above their circumstances. The ones left alone to raise their selves are the ones to fall from innocence. Bad behavior must suffer the consequences, or it will be repeated again and again. Parents are responsible for their children's discipline.

The children that are made when my sperm enters Alice's egg will know true love, not just a lustful moment. I will talk to them daily and rub Alice's belly so they know love every day of their existence. I will make time in my life for them, and they will be better people in the end because they know true love and all the power that goes with it.

I know I can't control everything life can throw at you, but I have all the control over my actions. How I respond, to my children's needs, will mold their future morals and outcome of how they live their life. I want to give them the tools to have the best life possible. I want to give them love and guidance as the foundation in their life.

I imagine my family with Alice all the time. It's as if they are already here. Two boys and three girls, playing in a large backyard, swinging on a tire swing, playing ball and jumping rope. It is just so real. With the other women I've been with, my thoughts were only about when I would get instant gratification again. It was all centered on lust and pleasure.

My thoughts for gratification with Alice are just as strong only in a sweet way. It's almost like I can smell sweet honeysuckle with my thoughts of Alice. With other women, there is no smell, just a heavy need to perform an act for relief. Afterwards it is as if I feel empty. The emptiness is what lust leaves you with, no future. Drugs have this same effect on me, the craving is overwhelming, and afterwards I'm left empty. This is how evil leaves you feeling.

I don't know why it took me so long to grow up and realize how much good and evil can rule your life, but I blame no one but myself. I chose the empty life of beautiful women and drugs and now I chase after my new life of Alice and the American dream. All I need is for Alice to say, "I do."

Alice has all the room she needs to make the decision of commitment for the future. She has to get past the fear that is only in her imagination. What I have to offer her is everything she has ever dreamed of, a lifetime partner.

The more room I give Alice, the stronger her advances become. I vow not to get weak and give in to my feelings. I tell myself how special our wedding night will be because I stayed strong. Alice will always remember our wedding night and when she does, a smile will come across her face.

Tonight I will ask Alice to marry me again but first, I will let her tell me what she expects from the man she marries, whoever he may be.

I hear Alice's car pulling into the driveway and I open the door to go out and greet her. I said, "Alice, you're early, what a pleasant surprise."

Alice said, "I just couldn't wait to see you. It's been two days and I miss you something awful."

I said, "Let's go to the backyard and I'll start up the grill, it's a beautiful day for cooking outside. Go ahead and make yourself comfortable and I'll fix us some tea. There is a blanket on the ground under the oak tree; I thought we would have a picnic. You know, get close to nature."

Alice sat on the blanket, took the clip out of her hair, threw her head back and gazed at the clouds drifting in the sky. Her hair laid on her bare shoulders like vines of honeysuckle with soft blossoms that I can smell through the window, that's the effect Alice has on me. It's amazing.

As I walk out the back door with ice tea in my hands, Alice raises her arms and asks me to give her a kiss. I set the glasses on the picnic table, take her hands, lower my body and lock my lips on hers. My body is melting into Alice as we roll on the blanket. Her breasts and hips are like burning cinders that need hosing down before they start burning out of control. We are being naughty, like teenagers learning about how their bodies work. I'm losing control as Alice becomes the aggressor, and I'm too weak to fight her off. Alice begins to kiss my neck with her moist lips and my body becomes mush, except for my manhood.

Alice presses her body against mine uncontrollably and tells me she needs me more than she knew possible. My desire for Alice is climbing higher and higher with the sweet words, she is whispering in my ear; I'm to the point I can hardly breathe. As I run my fingers through her long beautiful hair, I pull Alice's lips to mine for one final kiss and I jump to my feet before I cross the line.

Alice extended her hand for me to help her to her feet.

Alice said, "Do you need any help grilling the burgers?"

I said, "Today I'm cooking for you, but please sit at the picnic table, I'll be right back with a glass of wine for you."

I grabbed the blanket off the ground and scurried into the house. I smelled the blanket and Alice's scent was all over it. I gave it a hug and threw it on the bed.

Alice said, "Oh thank you Ed, a glass of red wine is just what I need right now, it takes the edge off. I kind of got carried away, in a nice sort of way. I'm glad you have a wooden privacy fence, we needed it, don't you think."

I said, "Yes indeed we did. We got lost in the moment. By the way, Alice, how are you feeling about our relationship? Are we making progress?"

Alice said, "Yes we are. I'm more comfortable with you than I ever thought I would be. You know we just got carried away on the blanket and your foreplay left me breathless. If you were the kind of guy to take advantage of that, you could have had me. I was completely powerless under your spell.

Ed I don't like any kinky stuff, what I like in a relationship is a lot of foreplay until I can no longer control myself. Working myself up until I can't hold out any longer is what makes waiting for sex work for me. I know you are perfect for me in that department, my question is, can you be satisfied with what we just experienced, or only by completing the act? On my wedding night I will cross the line to total bliss."

I said, "Alice, I'm complete just being in a room with you, but if we are to have a family, completing the act is a must. Any way you want it will excite me at a level I have never been before. The kinky stuff is for people who don't have the excitement we have for each other. Alice, I will never lose my excitement for you, therefore, I will never need kinky. You are all I can possibly dream of."

Alice said, "That's good. I need control of what happens in the lovemaking department. The off the wall things make me feel like I am being degraded, I wish I wasn't such a prude when it comes to kinky, but I am."

I said, "Alice, you lead me anywhere you want, once we are married. I'm yours to do with as you please."

Alice sipped her wine as I put the burgers on the grill. I can feel her eyes on me and my body burns with joy. We are making progress; the conversation is all about our future.

Alice said, "Ed, you know I've been reading the Bible a lot lately, I'm starting to see what you see in this book. The guidance in the Bible is all a person needs to live the good life. I can hardly put it down. I wake up in the morning with the Bible lying on my chest where I fell asleep reading. Ed, I think I want to be saved; heaven is where I want to wind up for eternity. I thank you for introducing me to God. My eyes are open to my purpose in life, thanks to you."

I said, "Alice that means everything to me. I want to hear you give yourself to God right this moment. It will mean everything to me."

Alice said, "This moment has more meaning for me than anything in my entire life. My heart is so full of God's existence and I want to share the moment I give myself to Jesus. My heart is bursting with joy, the joy only Jesus can bring. The Bible talks about the joy wine can bring, I'm pouring this wine on the ground because right now all I need is the joy of the Word. It is all around me. I am asking God to save me, my eyes are open to your love and I accept everything you are giving me. I accept Your salvation, God. Let me walk in your light."

I said, "This is the best day of my life Alice, I witnessed you giving yourself to our Lord Jesus Christ. My life is now complete."

Alice said, "How can my parents be so blind. I followed their teachings and always felt empty. Now I know why. My creator was left out of my life."

I said, "You know Alice, I felt today would be special, it turns out to be more than special, it's spiritual. I couldn't ask for a more perfect day."

Alice said, "You know I've been reading the Bible for some time now, getting to know God the way you do Ed, but today He has entered my life and I feel Him in my soul. I feel so complete and full, words can't explain what is going on with me right this moment."

My thoughts of asking Alice to marry me will have to wait for another day, what has happened today needs no distractions.

The burgers are done and I bring them to the table as Alice pours us some water to wash them down with.

Alice said, "Ed would you add a extra slice of tomato to my burger? Thanks, that's just perfect. I never can get enough tomato on my sandwich. You are such a good cook.

You know Ed, I've always thought of love as someone who is having a mental breakdown because they actually lose their mind, but now that God has opened my mind to Himself I understand love completely. Love is trusting in God for everything. It is having faith.

I always compared love to what I have seen my friends going through. When my friends go through a break-up, the light goes out of their eyes; they look like the walking dead, like zombies.

The way I see it right this minute, with God in my heart, no matter what happens in life, I will always have the light of God in my heart. Ed, you could walk out of my life right now and I would be okay with it. God will protect my heart.

When you die, you face God alone. The people, who try to drag you away from God, will not be there. I say, get away from them as fast as you can."

Alice has opened her eyes today and realized that lust never satisfies you; you die spiritually. God opened Alice's eyes today and I was a witness to the event. I am so blessed.

I said, "I will never leave you Alice, I'm deeply in love with you now and always."

Alice said, "Ed you are the strongest willed man I've ever known. When you stopped us from going too far, is when I had my epiphany. God opened my eyes when he protected you from a lustful heart. When you pulled away and grabbed the blanket off the ground and stormed into the house, all I could feel was sweetness like I've never experienced in my entire life. I figure it must be God Himself protecting us from our desires. I think He has something much better in mind for us. From now on I will be listening to God and acting according to His will."

When Alice came to my house today I planned to ask her to marry me with a very stern voice, however today is God's day with Alice and I intend to give them all the space they need to get to know each other. Alice has that light, that twinkle that people get when they give their life to God. No way can I interrupt Alice while she is walking in God's light for the first time in her life. God has given me the mental discipline to know when to step aside.

What I planned to say to Alice today is, 'The feelings I get from you are stronger than any drug I have ever done. If you love me like you do right now for the rest of my life, I will never look at another woman. I know you love me because I can feel what you feel. All I need in this life is your love, nothing else matters. I don't want just your sex, I want your love. There is radiance around you, full of love, which is the part of Alice that I want. Do you understand?

I wear no disguise in my personality, what you see is what you get. The favor of God is upon me and that is how I found you Alice.'

Anyway, that is what I had planned to say today. It will just have to wait for another day; today Alice is being introduced to God.

Alice said, "You know Ed, all my life I took it for granted that my parents were right about the whole God thing. You know they have never read the Bible, yet they discard it as having no meaning. Ed, you have opened my eyes to the importance of the Word, and how the Word has been playing out for the last two thousand years. Everything in the Old Testament is telling you about the New Testament's future. It's amazing."

I said, "You are right. If you want to know what is in store for the future, the Bible will tell you, if you just read God's Word.

I received a message from God while reading His word in Genesis 6:5-6 "And God saw that the wickedness of man was great in the earth, and that every imagination of the thoughts of his heart was only evil continually. 6And it repented the Lord that he had made man on the earth, and it grieved him at his heart." The life I was living was full of wickedness and I was dying in spirit and flesh. I was destroying myself just like God destroyed the wicked world with the floods. I made a train wreck out of my life, now I'm salvaging what is left of it, and giving it to God to do with as He wills. By doing this I have discovered the true meaning of life, 'love.' It is pure, it is good, and I now have true happiness. God sent me you, He has turned my world upside-down and I have so much grace in my heart that I will never stray from the teachings of the Bible. Now He has opened your eyes Alice, we have a bright future together. Alice, we were made for each other, by God's hands. God has given me the Spirit of Wisdom."

Chapter 18
A Visit from Chelsea

Jeff spent the entire day cleaning the house, mowing the lawn, sweeping the back patio and buying groceries. His friend Chelsea Songbird is stopping for a day on her way home to Tahlequah, Oklahoma. College is out for a week and she is lonesome for her family. Chelsea is a great kid and we try to make her visit as pleasant as possible.

Jeff said, "There she is pulling into the driveway. Let's help her with the bags."

When Chelsea got out of the car, she gave Jeff a big hug and told him how much she missed him. She waved me over to join in for a group hug. Sweetness filled the air as I took a deep breath.

Chelsea said, "Guys, I want to show you something. Close your eyes while I get him out of the back seat. Okay, you can open your eyes now. This is Chick-a-Dee, my pet rooster. Isn't he beautiful?"

Jeff said, "His feathers are beautiful and his crow is loud. How are we supposed to sleep with this loud rooster?"

Chelsea said, "I put a cover over his pen and he sleeps like a baby. I'm going to take him out of his cage so he can stretch, do you mind?"

As the rooster was released, he began flying and landed on top of Chelsea's car. He began to flap his wings and crow. Freedom has Chick-a-Dee all excited.

Chelsea picks him up and he begins to sing the sweetest little song. She places him in the grass and he begins dancing in a circle, putting on a show. I must say he is a very fancy dancing bird.

I said, "May I pick him up?" Chelsea nodded a yes. "This chicken will make a great soup for lunch tomorrow."

Chelsea said, "No way, he is my pet. The only thing you can have is his waddles for a pepperoni pizza. I'm going to remove them so that this winter they don't freeze when he gets a drink of water. Oklahoma has a much colder winter season than Texas."

We went in the house, Chelsea headed for the back yard with her rooster, and Jeff was right behind her. She set the rooster down and he began to chase grasshoppers. I guess that is his lunch. After he filled his craw, he began scratching the grass until he hit dirt, then he took a dirt bath. Dirt was flying two feet into the air as Chick-a-Dee began to make a growling noise to let us know he was in heaven.

Jeff said, "He is right at home, why don't you let me have him and you just get another?"

Chelsea said, "No way, Chick-a-Dee is my pet. I really care about him."

Jeff said, "You can always visit him, maybe I would see you more often if he lived here. You would have twice the reason to come around."

These two went on and on with their game of who will end up with the rooster. I must say he looks happy here.

I promised Alice a call when Chelsea arrived so she can spend some quality time with her; the two of them somehow just click. I like to think there is a connection with the three of us.

Jeff is catching grasshoppers in the back yard and feeding them to Chick-a-Dee.

Chelsea said, "You are going to make him lazy.

160

Look at his craw; it is so full it's about to bust. If he took off running after a bug right now, he would probably fall on his face from being so top heavy. For some reason he just can't say no to you and the bugs."

About this time, Alice came through the back door and Chelsea grabbed her and gave her a big hug.

Alice said, "It is so good to see you; college really agrees with you, everything about you looks mature and wholesome at the same time. I want to know everything that you have been up to, in school and out of school."

Chelsea said, "Have a seat and I will begin right now. Well Alice, I have a school project that is requiring documentation of a brown thrasher bird building a nest and laying eggs. You know a brown thrasher is a very shy bird so this has become a difficult task. I dress in camouflage and sit very still while I film. One day I wanted to see how many eggs were in the nest so I waited until the bird was off the nest to get a peek. Suddenly two brown thrashers were attacking the top of my head. Two eggs were in the nest and I never went near the nest again. I filmed from a distance and just zoomed in on them. Both eggs hatched and I watched as the mother and father took great care of them. The area where the nest was had thick brush so I would look for something moving like a leaf or branch and then look for the brown thrasher. They blend in so well with nature that if you blink you will miss them. I choose this project because of the story you told about the brown thrasher you thought you saw, that turned out to be a leaf. You were so excited when you thought it was a bird. I wanted to feel that excitement an now I know what you were talking about. It is truly a thrill to see one. "

Alice said, "That sounds like a very fun project. What I want to know now is, are you dating anyone special?"

Chelsea said, "I date a lot but no one special. Friendship dates only. No one has caught my eye like Jeff or Zack. Don't get me wrong, there are some good guys in college and I belong to a club called Birding, where we take our binoculars and walk through the woods looking at birds. It reminds me of home, and of Zack; he would love this new sport. Total silence while you are walking with a group of rowdy college students. It's kind of neat to be in total silence with your date, you learn a lot about emotions and control."

Alice said, "Well I guess a long walk in the woods agrees with you, fresh is the word I'm looking for; you look refreshed."

Chelsea said, "I may look refreshed Alice, but you have a glow of happiness about you, what is going on?"

Alice said, "Just between you and me, I'm in love with Ed. I know it is love because he consumes my every thought. My body is full of joy like I never knew existed. My only fear is that what goes up must come down. You just can't fly high like this for a lifetime."

Chelsea said, "Why not?"

Alice said, "It is impossible to feel this good for a lifetime. I know no one who is able to hold on to this kind of joy. In fact, I know no one who is full of the kind of joy Ed brings to me every day of my life. It's what people describe as heaven on earth.

I have started reading the Bible so I can understand this kind of joy. That is some Book; it speaks of every kind of emotion the human body will experience. I have learned so much about life by reading the Word of God. God is the Word and the Word is God. They are the same. The whole thing blows my mind. I wish my parents were believers so I would have read it when I was young. I feel I missed a lot in life.

Chelsea, I want you to know that I now believe in God. My heart is so full of God I could bust. I pray every day. Prayer is the elevation of my mind connected with my creator. I never knew this peaceful feeling in my life. You see Chelsea; nothing is different until we think differently. My parents always bragged about creating me; I know now that God created me, the Bible tells me that. God knew me before my parents conceived me.

I love my parents but they are just wrong about the existence of God. Ed opened my eyes to God. When Ed would speak about how God changed his life, his pupils would take over his entire eyes. He would say, 'right believing will always produce right living.'

Chelsea, it is such a gift that I can talk to my creator anytime I want. God is guiding me in the right direction with Ed. I was trying to lead Ed in the wrong direction as Eve did Adam in the garden. I wanted Ed to make love to me to prove that he loved me. Marriage is much more than just sex. I know that now. Sex is a gift from God meant for marriage.

When Ed first got serious with me he would say, 'I don't want a starter wife like a starter house, I want a wife for a lifetime.' That makes good sense to me. When I would push to take our relationship to the next level of intimacy Ed would stop us and say, 'The devil cannot do anything to you unless you cooperate with him.' I would come to my senses immediately. This would be a sin and sin is temporary satisfaction, and the wages of sin is death to our relationship. You see there is a difference in pleasure and happiness; I refuse to let the Devil steal my lifetime of happiness for a moment of pleasure outside of marriage.

When I marry Ed our love will be yoked evenly, it will last a lifetime. I want what Ed wants now that I know God. We both have the ability to live above the sin of lust. Ed's famous line for that is, 'He who governs his passion is master of his world. You must ask God for what you want; the strength to say, not yet.'"

Chelsea said, "I'm so happy you and Ed are in love and not just in lust. You know when you mentioned your love would be yoked evenly, that impressed me more than anything you have ever said. Alice, Ed wants to marry you, even if you didn't believe in God, you know that. Because you found God, you have a shared purpose in life, to serve God. What a gift you will be giving your children. Your life together will be blessed."

Alice said, "I know Ed is in love with me and would marry me no matter what, but I have not said 'yes' to his request. I want to finish reading the Bible so I can be filled with the Holy Spirit and know God through His Word. So far, I see God in heaven and Jesus sitting at His right hand and the Holy Spirit on earth filling anyone's body who asks Him to enter them. He is like a whiff of air or a wind. That is how He enters me anyway.

I trust you will keep my secret, until I say 'yes' to marry Ed. I wanted to share my feelings with you because if not for you, Ed would not be the wonderful person he is today. He would still be that empty shell going from one woman to another. I know Jeff's accident played a roll also, but you Chelsea helped mold him into the Ed he is today"

A tear rolled down Alice's face as she gazed across the yard at Jeff holding Chick-a-Dee. Alice finally is able to bare her soul, which is so full of joy she could burst, actually, the dam has broken, and tears are now rolling out of her eyes, tears of joy.

Alice and Chelsea sit in silence as they get their emotions in check. This is a lot of information for Chelsea to process.

Jeff said, "Hello Alice, let me introduce you to my new friend, Chick-a-Dee. He belongs to Chelsea but he loves our back yard and I am trying to convince Chelsea to let him live here. Maybe you can convince her that I will be an excellent caretaker for her rooster. He let me pick him up and eats every bug I put in front of him."

Alice said, "I refuse to get into your business. Maybe

you can flip a coin."

Chelsea said, "No way. Chick-a-Dee is going to my home, my mother already has a hen picked out for him and I can't wait to see the baby chicks this spring."

I said, "Dinner is ready; backed chicken over rice, cornbread, salad and tea to drink. Jeff, you can put that rooster down, he looks like he is had plenty to eat."

After everyone washed up, Alice offered to say a prayer over dinner. This is the first time Alice has acknowledged God's existence in front of anyone but me. I tried to hide the shocked look on my face but it was too late. Alice was looking into my eyes when she made the offer. I nodded my head in a matter of acceptance to her offer.

Alice said, "Thank you Lord, for these thy gifts which we are about to receive from thy bounty, through Christ our Lord, Amen."

A big smile came across my face and Alice was beaming with joy. She just announced that she has found God. It's just like her to let me know through a prayer that she wants everyone to know, she has God in her heart.

After dinner, Alice and Chelsea volunteered to do the dishes. Jeff went outside and put Chick-a-Dee in his box. We all watched a movie and afterwards. The girls left to spend the night at Alice's house. Chelsea planned to leave early in the morning when she was fresh. Chelsea is not a fan of long trips in the dark by herself.

Chapter 19
Alice's Eyes are Open

The phone ringing woke me up and Alice was on the other end. A year ago I would be so annoyed that the phone would be ringing on a Sunday at 7:00 a.m., but just thinking it might be Alice cleared my head immediately. I answered as if I already had two cups of coffee and had been awake for an hour.

I said, "Good morning beautiful, so good to hear your voice."

Alice said, "Just wanted you to know Chelsea refused to call you this morning to tell you good-bye. She said you are not a morning person. I don't know if you can hear her or not, she is saying to tell you and Jeff that she had a great time yesterday and she is out the door."

I said, "Tell her 'bye' for me. She is accustomed to the old Ed, before you came into my life. The whole world is different with you in it. The ringing of the phone just wakes me up into Alice's world. The world where I want to spend the rest of my life; will you marry me Alice so my dream will come true, I love you beyond words."

Alice said, "We will see."

I said, "How about I pick you up and we go to church today. Your prayer before dinner yesterday was beautiful and I know God would love for you to visit his home."

Alice said, "I'm already dressed in my Sunday best so why don't you come over, I will get the coffee ready and cook you some eggs and bacon."

I said, "I won't be long."

As we were driving to church, Alice began to tell me she has been reading the Bible for several months. She talked about how the Old Testament predicted what the New Testament was about, 'This over two thousand year old book tells you everything about life.' She talked about how she always thought evil was the norm and righteousness was the exception. This is why we have so many manmade laws. They are to keep the devil in line. She sees that now.

Alice talked about her interpretation of the Bible and that God is not a sugar daddy, that when He gives you a favor, you need to thank Him, and ask what you can do for his people. Desire nothing on earth, take only what God gives you. No one deserves what God gives you, just accept it, be in the will of God. Just do all to the glory of God.

Alice knows more about the Bible than most people who have gone to church all their life. 'There is just something about reading the Word yourself,' she would say.

I'm so excited about Alice reading the Bible that butterflies are fluttering in my entire body. She must be thinking about marrying me, why else would she change her way of thinking. She wants to make our life whole. She knows I want to marry her without any changes. Alice made an effort to learn what is important to me in life and on the journey, she found God for herself. How great is that? She must be in love with me.

Alice is even talking about getting baptized. Through baptism, you become the temple of God, the voice of God.

I always told Alice that for the new me it will take three to make love; you, God and me. I think she understands what I meant now. Reading the Word of God has opened her eyes to what is important in my life; the joy of Jesus. The old me, who thought, lying at the speed of light to get what you want for instant gratification, no longer exists. I am on a mission for lasting love, a love of a lifetime, the love that God guides.

Unless we look inward we will never understand life, and I have God inside me to answer all my questions. Before living in the Word of God, I was always angry, and anger is just one letter away from danger. If I had continued on the road of self-pleasure, I would have died a lonely, angry young man. I no longer look left and right seeking pleasure from women and drugs; I look straight ahead, at God. I remember all of the traps that the devil set for me in the past, and that is where he will remain, in the past.

As the church draws nearer, Alice said, "What a beautiful home God lives in, I am so happy you invited me to this part of your life.   With God in my heart the church has a whole new look to it."

I said, "This is where we will get married."

Alice looked at me and raised one eyebrow. I think she was caught off guard, she was speechless. Alice gazed at the church with what I hoped was approval of where she would be walking down the aisle all dressed in white. Alice will make the most beautiful bride to ever walk down the steps of this church.

Alice said, "This is a quaint little church, I like it. Do you think the people I met will remember me. It's been awhile since I've been here?"

As we walked up the steps of the church, members once again noticed that I had a girl on my arm for the second time in all the Sundays that I have attended. The warm welcoming smiles made Alice feel special. She was beaming as members walked up to introduce themselves to the girl whose hand I was holding.

As we walked into the church to take our seats, Alice said, "They are a very warm but bold bunch."

I said, "They are real, nothing is phony about God's people."

The preacher began his sermon with the importance of Israel. "Jesus lived there. The temple mount is the Holiest place in the world. It is the holy mount of the House of the Lord, the place of the third temple. When God returns He will put His foot on the temple mount.

It would not matter who nailed Jesus to the cross, Romans or Jews, Christ is responsible for his death. He died for us. His death is our gift from God. Some day he will return to the temple mount and take us to heaven to live in God's kingdom. The people who do not accept God as their savior and choose to live in sin like Sodom and Gomorrah will burn in hell. Sodom and Gomorrah is the lowest place on earth, the closest to Hell. It is now called Jordan.

We are all sinners. Because Jesus died for our sins, when I sin, I cause Jesus pain. It is as if I am pushing the thorns on his head deeper. Just the thought of that pains my soul, so I make every effort to kick the devil out of my life. Yes, I am a preacher, but I am also a sinner. The Grace of God forgives me of my sins, and your sins.

The devil goes after a good person a lot harder than he does a sinner. He already has the person who lives his life in sin. The devil puts in overtime in the person who is trying to live a life of faith in God. The devil sets traps for you. If you don't stay on your toes, you will be in his trap before you even realize it.

Gentlemen, he could tempt you with a beautiful woman." Alice poked me in my side with her elbow. I could not help the grin that came across my face. "Men get aroused by what their eyes see. You have control over nature if you choose to use it. Ladies, he could tempt you with jealousy when your man looks at the beautiful woman." I poked Alice in her ribs and she could not control the grin that encompassed her whole face. "Ladies, you may be tempted to call your man a bad name or attack the beautiful woman, this is how the devil works. He looks for your weakness and exploits it. Do not give him the satisfaction of victory over your emotions. Take your mind to another place until you get control. The same goes for you gentlemen. Just ask God for the strength, that's what He is here for, to help us get to heaven."

What a sermon. I could tell Alice was impressed with the preacher. She had lightness in her step as we exited the church. She gave my hand a squeeze as the sunlight hit our faces.

Alice said, "I had no idea what I've been missing all these years. Your preacher is a real inspiration. I like how he tied Sodom and Gomorrah to the present times of men being womanizers. There is nothing new that wasn't going on two thousand years ago. In the Bible, they were having some real swinging parties. None of them got away with it and neither will our modern day Sodom and Gomorrah evil doers. You will pay in the here and now or the hereafter. I'm so glad you repented Ed, and I'm so glad I met you and you introduced me to God. Denying God's existence is the worst sin you can commit, that is why it is the first commandment. It says so in the Bible. I've asked God to forgive me and I felt Him come into my heart. I had the palms of my hand raised to heaven and He entered through my hands and into my entire body. It was amazing."

I said, "Alice, I'm so proud you shared your experience with me. I've been praying for you to find God, I guess He is listening to me. Now I'm going to share with you how I've always known God but refused to follow all the good advice He has always given me. Before I let God rule my life, I was always angry. Drugs were my way of dealing with all the anger. It was a losing situation."

The preacher came outside to mingle with the church members. Everyone seemed to enjoy talking with him.

Alice just held my hand and watched how everyone enjoyed each other's company. He definitely has a way with words; his people love him.

Alice said, "Ed, I would like our preacher to baptize me and wash away all my sins. I really like him. I would like to be baptized next Sunday."

I said, "Our preacher, does that mean you want to join this church?"

Alice said, "Absolutely, I feel like I've been going here all my life. I fit in."

My heart is bursting with joy; I feel one-step closer to living the rest of my life with Alice. I called the preacher over and introduced him to Alice once again, and explained how she wanted to join the church and get baptized next week. The preacher agreed on baptism next week when Alice explained she has read the entire Bible; however, Alice will need to take instructions on the church values while she is becoming a member of the church.

I could feel the excitement in the air as I drove Alice home.

Alice said, "Our church feels like God's home. It is small and humble just as I imagine Jesus to be. I felt like I was in heaven when I walked into His home, like the images in the stained glass windows that are so beautiful and tell the story of who He is with all His glory. I can't believe it took me this long to find Him.

The United States of America was founded on the principles of freedom of religion. I was brought up to believe I had a choice, to believe whatever I wanted to believe, but I was influenced by my atheist parents. They always made fun of religion and people who believed.

The system created for the United States of America has lasted over two-hundred and forty years. No other system in the world can compare to the freedom we have.

Ed, you opened my eyes to God and I thank you

for doing that. I look at God and country in a completely different light now. My eyes are open to the importance of what America was founded on because now I know God, the Bible opened my heart.

'In God we trust' is printed on our paper money. I have a new appreciation for those words, spoken and printed by our forefathers. The song, 'God Bless America' is in my heart, sometimes when I hear it sung the feeling is so strong I well-up with tears.

I do not blame my parents for influencing me. My grandparents were also atheist and taught my parents their beliefs; I plan to break the generational curse and raise my children in the church."

As we drove along Alice began to hum one of the songs we sang in church. She is so content that I can feel the peacefulness God has blessed upon her. It's just another blessing God is sending my way.

I wonder what Alice's parents will think about her conversion to Christianity. People can only give what they have; you can't give what you don't have, or teach what you don't know. No parent is perfect and they all scar their children. You must forgive them.

Alice said, "I committed to memory a verse in the Bible that stole my heart. It is in Philippians 2:2-3 'Fulfil ye my joy, that ye be likeminded, having the same love, being of one accord, of one mind. Let nothing be done through strife or vainglory; but in lowliness of mind let each esteem other better than themselves.' It is so like what you are Ed. I understand what you are all about. You want our love to be yoked evenly. There is a natural body and a spiritual body, and you have progressed to the latter. I finally get it. Talking to God is like having a friendly conversation with someone you love. Prayer is just talking to God. I had been restless until I let my heart rest in God; I now know peace.

I am ashamed of how I tried to arouse you to a lustful

breaking point. You want better for us. I've always thought that 'yoked evenly' meant that a couple looks to be on the same plain. Now that I have read the Bible, I know that 'yoked evenly' means you both believe in God. I am now in the spiritual realm that you rest in. Oh Ed, I am so happy I now understand the depth of your love. I want to go to heaven with you. There is nothing in heaven but love.

I always thought I could never hold you for a lifetime because I'm ugly. I just wanted to taste your love so I could savor it for a lifetime. My jealous nature chokes me every time a beautiful woman looks at you; now I understand that it is the devil putting a wedge between our hearts. In the future, if that happens, I will speak to the devil and condemn him. I will break him with the words you use; I will tell him that Ed thinks I am beautiful and that is all that matters in our world. I will talk the devil out of my mind."

I said, "I should have taken you to church the day I met you."

Alice said, "No Ed, things have worked out perfectly. Church would never have grabbed a hold of me like it did if I had not read the Bible. The Word is what opened my mind, and God's house embraced my heart. It was all in God's plan for our future."

I said, "Alice, marry me."

She just looked at me with a big smile on her face. We pulled into her driveway and when we got out of the car, Alice embraced me and kissed me in a different way. It was the sweetest kiss I have ever enjoyed. No lust, just sweetness; something has come over Alice; she is in a different world.

I watched as she prepared dinner with lightness in her step and a song on her breath.

The evening was like we were floating on air. We were both in a place neither has ever been. When it was time for me to go home, I asked one more time, "Alice, will you marry me?"

Alice said, "Yes, yes, yes I will marry you, my love."

The End